EXECU

CARFANO CRIME FAMILY
BOOK 4

REBECCA GANNON

newsletter, blog, shop, and links to all social media:
www.rebeccagannon.com

CONTENT WARNING
This book is intended for readers 18 and older due to its explicit mature nature. It has references to childhood trauma and contains scenes of graphic violence that may pose as a trigger or make some readers uncomfortable.

More by Rebecca Gannon

Pine Cove
Her Maine Attraction
Her Maine Reaction
Her Maine Risk
Her Maine Distraction

Carfano Crime Family
Casino King
The Boss
Vengeance
Executioner
Wild Ace

Standalone Novels
Whiskey & Wine
Redeeming His Reputation

To those who feel their life isn't in their control,
may you find the strength to find your way, on your terms.
You have more power than you realize.
This is for you.

THE CARFANO FAMILY

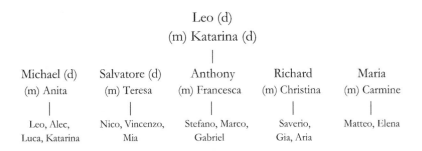

Leo (d)
(m) Katarina (d)

Michael (d)	Salvatore (d)	Anthony	Richard	Maria
(m) Anita	(m) Teresa	(m) Francesca	(m) Christina	(m) Carmine
Leo, Alec, Luca, Katarina	Nico, Vincenzo, Mia	Stefano, Marco, Gabriel	Saverio, Gia, Aria	Matteo, Elena

(m) – married / (d) – deceased

it was as if she was born into this world
invisible & he was the first one to notice her —
to truly see her. after a lifetime of dancing with
her own shadow, she'd found someone who
could keep in perfect time with her.

finally, finally.

— the ~~un~~seen girl.

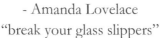

- Amanda Lovelace
"break your glass slippers"

CHAPTER 1
Dante

Holding my phone tightly, I watch Katarina walk the perimeter of the yard. I zoom in and see her beautiful face marred with sadness, and anger surges through me.

What the fuck happened?

With a gust of wind, she crosses her arms over her middle to fend off the bitter bite of the air, then swipes at her cheek.

Another wave of anger has me about to crush my phone in my hand.

She shouldn't cry. Ever.

No one is worth her tears.

If I could give her any guarantee, it's that whoever hurts

her will always be met with the blade of my knife or the barrel of my gun.

Katarina Carfano is mine.

She's been mine since I allowed myself to want her.

Her father brought me into his home when I was thirteen, and Katarina was only six. She took one look at me and her little eyes widened in fear before she ran upstairs to hide in her room.

She was right to hide from me then, but now there's nowhere she can go that I wouldn't find her. I've watched her grow into the woman she is, memorizing everything about her. I know her better than anyone. She may think she hides behind that mask she wears for everyone, but I see everything. I know every move she makes. Her body tells the story she refuses to let anyone know.

It's taken everything in me to not fucking claim her every day that I've been breathing since she turned eighteen. That was four years ago, and the only way I've been able to hold back is by doing my job. But also knowing that if I did have her, then Leo — the head of the family and her oldest brother — would fucking kill me himself while her other two brothers, Alec and Luca, looked on.

It wouldn't matter that we went to school together, trained together, took beatings together, and lived under the same roof. Their father, Michael Carfano, told me I owed him a debt that could, and would, only be paid with my life, and that I was to be the protector of his children at all costs, no matter what. Although, I think taking his precious daughter and dirtying her with my sins isn't what he had in mind when he said to protect her.

My phone starts vibrating with a call from Leo, blocking my view of Katarina on the security camera feed.

Grinding my jaw, I unclench it and huff out, "Boss."

"We have a meeting with the Antonuccis on Saturday. I need you to coordinate the men."

"Where is it?"

"Giorgio's. Prepare the same as you did for the Cicariello meeting. I don't want any surprises with them. They might want to make a show of power for what we're meeting about."

"Which is?"

"Katarina," he says after a beat, and my vision blurs.

"What about Katarina?" I ask roughly, trying not to let my rage be known.

"We're discussing her union with Santino."

Red. I see red. Blood fucking everywhere as my mind flashes through every conceivable way I will kill Santino Antonucci.

They want to marry her off to that fucker when he's as weak as his father and grandfather, and nowhere near good enough for Katarina. No one is.

"I'll take care of everything," I grunt out.

Yeah, I'll take care of everything, but I'm also going to be standing right there to look those pussies in their eyes to show them exactly who's coming for them.

CHAPTER 2
Dante

Everyone's in position.

We had a meeting here last month when we had to broker a deal with Dom and Geno Cicariello for their sister Angela, Luca's woman. And the meeting went just about as good as expected where two assholes who have zero respect for their sister are concerned.

I had two teams of men make the sweep of the surrounding blocks this morning for anyone the Antonuccis may have tried to set up for an ambush, and then had them take their posts around Giorgio's building and across the street for security.

Cracking my neck, I roll my shoulders back and punch in

the security code for the elevator, riding down to the garage. If I make it through this meeting without killing anyone, I'll call it a success.

"Ready to go?" Leo asks when I step off the elevator. His driver and bodyguard, Alfie, is standing quietly beside him. I give him a sharp nod and we climb into the blacked-out Range Rover. "Luca and Alec are in the cars behind us," he informs me.

"All of you? Is that a good idea?"

"We all get a say in what happens with Kat."

My fists ball at my sides, keeping my face neutral. "Does she know?"

"Not yet. We're waiting until after today to talk with her. Everyone's in place?"

"Yes," I confirm, my tone clipped. "Nothing out of the ordinary. We're good." I can feel his eyes slide over to me, but he doesn't say anything.

No one questions me. No one asks me why I am the way I am or why I do or say what I do, and that's the way I like it. I may take orders, but I don't *ever* fucking explain myself.

Pulling up to Giorgio's, I do a visual sweep of the street and lead the way inside. All three sit on one side of the rectangular table facing the door, and I take my position behind them, standing beside Alfie and two of my best men.

A few minutes later, a car pulls up outside, and Frank and Santino step out. Giuseppe Antonucci is still the head of the family, but at his advanced age, he lets his first born son, Frank, do most of the duties.

"Frank and Santino. Welcome," Leo greets, and he, Luca, and Alec stand to shake their hands.

5

Frank nods. "It's good to finally have a face-to-face with you since you've taken over for your father."

"If you wanted one sooner, you could've asked," Leo states simply.

"Michael and I made arrangements for Santino and Katarina to be wed after she turned 18."

"That was never brought up to me before he was killed, and you've had five years to come to me," Leo challenges.

Frank narrows his eyes. "What are you trying to say?"

"Why did you wait so long to contact me for this meeting?"

"Jesus, Leo," he grinds out. "I didn't want my son and family caught in the middle of your revenge plot with the Cicariellos."

No one says anything, but I know what they're thinking. *Pussies.* Like Leo would ever ask or involve another family to fight in a battle that's ours to fight.

"It's over now," Frank continues. "You've taken care of them and you've done plenty to prove yourself worthy of taking over for Michael."

Leo doesn't respond right away, the air in the room thick with tension. "I may have taken my father's place, but I'm not him. I'm not handing my sister over to a man I don't know or trust."

Handed over to.

My blood is fucking racing through my veins right now. She's not a *thing* to be handed over. She's the fucking sun and moon — above us all and untouchable.

With a nod, Frank clears his throat. "I'm prepared to merge our trucking company with yours. We'll both double our profits." Pulling out an envelope from his inner suit jacket pocket, he slides it across the table to Leo. "Those are our numbers."

Leo doesn't even bother touching the envelope. "I already know your numbers," he tells him. "I'll agree to the merger, so long as you know Katarina will always have our protection. She's a Carfano, even if she bears the Antonucci name."

"Understood. But as her husband, Santino will protect her." I look Santino over, knowing he would never do as good a job as me.

"Is that right? Will you protect her, Santino?" Leo questions, leaning forward.

Santino's gaze moves between all three brothers. "Yes."

"Because you know what would happen to you if you let anything happen to her, right?"

"I can imagine," the smartass says, making me want to kill him right fucking now.

"As long as we're clear. Which brings me to my next question. Where would you plan on living? What kind of security do you have?"

"I bought a brownstone a few years ago but haven't done anything with it. I thought it would be best to let my wife choose everything." He's sounding like a real fucking prick right now. As if Katarina is only good for decorating, and it'll keep her occupied while he works. She's meant for so much more than that. "And of course, I have top notch security there. She'll always be safe, even when I'm not there."

"Good." Leo nods, and it's making me want to knock

him the fuck out, which is a thought I've never had before. "So what will Katarina do? If you're working, what will she be doing?"

Santino looks momentarily stunned by the question. Abrianna, Leo's woman, runs a charity. Tessa, Alec's woman, is a dancer in a show at the family's casino and a dance teacher at a studio. And Angela, Luca's woman, will be going back to university for the Spring semester to finish her Art History degree.

It seems Santino is baffled by the idea of Katarina actually *doing* something.

"Uhm," he says like an idiot. "She'll make the house her own, and then when we have kids, she'll be a great mom."

I'm shaking with how angry I am right now, holding it in. If I move, it'll be to pull my gun out and shoot him in the head. If I open my mouth, it'll be to tell everyone in the room that no one is having kids with Katarina but me.

This piece of shit wants to make a good little homemaker housewife out of Katarina without even knowing her or knowing if that's what she wants.

"Of course she will be," Leo agrees, and I feel my skin get hot with the effort I'm putting into restraining myself. "And if she wanted to do something other than be a mother?"

This guy looks like that's such an odd concept, but he covers it up quickly. "Then we'll talk about it."

"Alright, let's meet next Saturday with Katarina."

"I'm looking forward to meeting her." Frank smiles, and it comes off as forced. "As is my son. Right, Santino?"

He flashes us a slick grin. "Yes, I am."

Flexing my hands, it takes every ounce of control I have to hold back from wiping that grin from his pretty-boy face in a single blow.

"Alright then, we'll see you back here next Saturday. Perhaps over a meal? I've heard good things about this place."

"Of course," Leo agrees. "We'll be celebrating."

Frank and Santino stand, and it isn't until after they leave that I dare move a muscle, taking slow, deliberate breaths to regain my control.

"He looks like a fucking prick," Alec spits out.

"She might like him," Luca offers, trying to be optimistic. "When are we going to tell her?"

"Tomorrow. I want her to have the week to get used to the idea."

Over my dead fucking body will Katarina marry that asshole.

She's mine.

She's *been* mine.

CHAPTER 3
Katarina

My brothers are driving me insane.

All three of them are bossy, overbearing, unrelenting, thickheaded men that have taken their roles as older brothers to a new level.

Since my father and uncle's deaths just over five years ago, Leo has taken his place as the head of the family, with Luca as his underboss and Alec running our family's casino in Atlantic City. And me? I'm still the little sister they feel the need to control and treat like an afterthought.

I'm twenty-two, not two, but it doesn't matter to them. To them, I have and always will be, the baby sister they need to protect and handle like a fragile porcelain doll.

I'm shocked they've been able to land the most amazing women that willingly put up with them, but they have, and now that they're coupled up, it seems they've put their sights on me.

I know that's what this meeting today is going to be about, and I'm already feeling the weight of defeat on my chest for whatever future I so stupidly thought I could have.

It doesn't matter. It's never mattered.

Jimmy, my driver and bodyguard I've had since I was fifteen, is driving me from my home on Staten Island where I live with my mother, to my family's building in Manhattan where my brothers live and work.

Pulling into the private underground parking garage, I close my eyes and take a moment for myself. For some reason, I feel like it's going to be one of the last I have before my brothers tell me I have to do what I've known I'm supposed to do for years now — marry someone for the family. Not for love, but for the family.

Most of the women born into the world I live in have to do it, my mother included. I don't want to end up like her, though. My father was an asshole on a good day, and treated her like a piece of property. A piece of shitty property that he didn't want for any other reason than children and a merger between two families.

I don't want that. I refuse to have that be the rest of my life.

"We're here, Miss Katarina," Jimmy says to me from the driver's seat.

With my eyes still closed, I sigh. "Yes, I know. I'm just preparing myself for what I know is about to happen."

"I'm sure it won't be too bad," he appeases, but we both already know what I'm walking into.

"It will. But I'm ready." Solidifying my resolve, I easily let my face go devoid of what I'm feeling, and practice the smile I've perfected over the years. I've gotten so good at it, that sometimes I even make myself believe I'm fine. I use it around my family so they see the happy little sister they think I am, and that's how I prefer it.

I'd rather be underestimated. That way, I come as a surprise when it's thought that I'll go down quietly. Then I'll be heard.

Climbing out of the car, I smooth my hands down the skirt of my dress to make sure everything's in place and raise my chin, walking confidently.

Jimmy punches in the code for the elevator, and when we step inside and the doors slide closed, I stare at my reflection in the polished metal, brutally aware of the girl staring back at me.

She looks put together. *She* looks like she has it all.

But *she* is neither of those things, while also being both of those things.

The elevator doors slide open again to the offices in the building, and walking down the hall, I see all three of my brothers at the conference table through the glass doors.

Taking a deep breath, I pull my shoulders back and breeze through the door like I don't have a care in the world.

"Hi, my dear brothers," I greet with my practiced smile in place. Resting my bag on the table, I leave a chair between myself and Luca empty, and sit in the next one. Leo is at his place at the head of the table, with Luca on one side and Alec on the other. "You summoned me?"

"We asked you here," Luca corrects, and I shoot him a look, then smile sweetly.

"Oh, right, of course. So, why was I *asked* here?"

Leo clears his throat. "It's been a few months since your twenty-second birthday, and it's time we discuss a couple things."

Still smiling, I say in a positive tone opposite of my true feelings, "You've already made it clear that I won't be traveling, I won't be moving to the city to be closer to Gia and Aria, and I won't be dating. Is there something else you want to add to that list?"

I wanted to move to Manhattan to be closer to my cousins, Gia and Aria, who are models with a big agency. They get to travel, go out, have fun, and meet guys. I wanted that too, but Leo wasn't having it. He told me I was too exposed on my own and that the easiest way someone could get to him was through me. Because, you know, he's more important than my happiness.

I don't even want to revisit his reaction to finding out I was talking to someone on the internet through a dating site a few months ago. He and my brothers threatened to have my internet monitored like a child if I didn't promise to never try that sneaky shit again.

I was feeling rebellious though, so I messaged the guy again, but he was quick to tell me he met someone else. We were only talking for a little over two weeks, but I was so mad at being dismissed like I was nothing, that I deleted the app and gave up. He wasn't even who I wanted anyhow.

"Katarina," Leo warns, and I grind my teeth together.

They all do this. All three of them. They're always saying my name as a warning, to be careful and to watch what I say next, and I hate it. I love them for the big, scary, over protective brothers that they are because I know they would do anything for me, but I hate feeling like I'm being censored. Like they don't want to even hear me speak.

It's time I drop all niceties and pretenses, and my smile fades. "Don't do that. Stop treating me like a little kid that needs pacifying. Just tell me why I'm here."

All three of them look at me for a silent beat before Leo speaks. "Alright. We met with Frank and Santino Antonucci yesterday," he tells me, and my hands grip the arms of the chair — the only outward sign of how I'm feeling. "If father was still alive, he'd have already done this when you turned 18."

Yes, I know.

"You're selling me to the highest bidder," I concede. "What do they have that you want? I want to know what my price tag looks like."

"Cut it out, Kat," Leo berates. "No one's fucking selling you. You're our sister and none of us are father. We would never let you be with a man who would treat you the way mom was. You're a Carfano. That means you hold the same power as all of us."

"Then why do I have to do this at all?"

"Because it's our job to find you someone. It's our job to make sure you're cared for. You can't marry outside of this world, Katarina. That's not how this works."

"Why not? You three were able to choose. I want to choose, Leo," I tell him, rubbing my chest.

"You might like him."

I choke out a humorless laugh. There's only one man I want, and he's not even an option. Never has been. "I doubt that." Standing, I push the chair back behind me with force and it hits the glass. "When is this meeting happening?"

"Saturday."

Anger surges through me, but I remain as calm as possible while my life spirals out of what semblance of control I had over it. "I'm warning you now," I say, pausing to look at each of them, "I can't promise to be as nice then as I'm being right now."

They remain silent as I storm off, with Jimmy coming out of nowhere to follow behind me.

I press the elevator button frantically like it'll magically show up faster, and tap my foot restlessly, praying to whoever is listening that none of them come after me right now.

The elevator finally dings and I blow out a rush of air in relief. But when the doors slide open, my heart completely stops for a moment before taking off double-time.

Dark, almost black eyes clash with mine, and I'm frozen in place. They penetrate me like lasers to my core, burning me and branding me so my insides are marked with him. Only him.

"Katarina." His voice is gruff, like my name is the first thing he's said all day, and yet it's still soothing to my frayed nerves.

I tighten my hold on my purse, trying to ground myself. "Dante," I manage to get out, all of my resolve from back in that room with my brothers gone like smoke in the wind.

"What's wrong?" he asks, his eyes never wavering from mine.

No one ever sees past what I want to show them, but he always seems to. Around him, I've never been able to keep my mask up. One look from him and he shatters it, leaving me open for scrutiny.

"Nothing," I say automatically, and his eyes squint just the slightest, calling out my lie. "My brothers," I start, then pinch my lips together. I don't even want to say it out loud.

A chill runs down my spine when his black eyes turn cold and distant before their focus returns, as if another person took over for a moment.

"I have to go," I say quickly, finally casting my eyes away from his to study my shoes.

Dante steps out of the elevator and I can feel his eyes on me as I duck inside, with Jimmy right behind me. It isn't until the doors are sliding closed again that I raise my gaze, meeting his head-on until the doors break our connection.

Shoving my purse into the crook of my elbow, I fold my arms across my chest and lean against the wall, closing my eyes. Every interaction I have with Dante leaves me needing to take a moment to put myself back together afterward. He disorients me in a way that I'm never prepared for, even when I know it's going to happen.

"I can't go home yet, Jimmy," I tell him when we're back in the car. "I don't want to face my mother and the million questions and opinions I'm sure she's going to bombard me with."

"Where would you like to go?" He must sense how I'm feeling because he normally wouldn't indulge me. We're not particularly close since he's only with me to perform his job, but there have been occasions where I've broken down in the back of the car after one family thing or another, and he's had to drive around until I'm calm enough to go home.

"Anywhere. I don't know. Just drive."

He gives me a curt nod in the rearview mirror and takes off. I look out the window, the buildings and people all blurring together after a while.

I already knew this was going to happen since I was fifteen and my father sat me down to discuss my place in the family as his daughter. *His only daughter.*

He told me it was my job to be a bridge between families when he needed it, and I was stupid enough to ask, *what if I didn't love him?*

I still remember the cold laugh he gave me, telling me it didn't matter if I loved him or not, and that I probably wouldn't. He said there's no room for love when you're a Carfano. He said love was just another word for weakness, and Carfanos aren't weak.

Now, I know I'm not weak, but I sure as hell feel weak right now. I feel defeated.

I'd like to believe my brothers wouldn't set me up with a complete monster. They may be assholes most of the time, but I know they love me. All I have to hold on to at the moment is hope. Hope that they'll give me a choice.

Although, the man I want to choose is completely off-limits to me and my brothers would never allow it.

I shouldn't want him.

Wanting him is a dangerous game I have no business playing, but it doesn't stop the fact that every time I'm near him, my body buzzes alive in a way it never has before, and in a way that scares me.

Dante Salerno is the epitome of 'stay away'. He doesn't smile. He rarely speaks. And his eyes will burn you with a single look while holding the depths of a lost soul drowning under the weight of a lifetime of pain and sins. To round out the 'stay away' air about him, he even has a scar that hooks down his jaw, starting from his right ear. It's a stark line through his short beard and a testament to the life he lives.

I was young when my father brought him into our home. I was only six and he was thirteen, and he scared me to death. I felt the pain and anger that seeped from him, so when I saw him, I ran.

From then on, I always ran into another room when he came into the one I was in, until the day I found myself feeling silly for being scared of a boy who had done nothing to me. My fear then morphed into curiosity, which then morphed into…I don't even know.

His eyes slid over me one day when I was fifteen or sixteen, and I felt them cover me like a caress of black velvet that left little pin pricks behind. Like he ran the soft petals of a black rose over my skin before rolling the stem of thorns over the same path.

The pain in his gaze was a welcome relief from feeling numb and unwanted my entire life. I suddenly felt seen.

Dante never went farther than studying me when I wasn't looking or thought I didn't know he was there. I always knew. I still know.

It wasn't until I was eighteen that I felt his touch for the first time. He brushed past me, his fingers sliding across my forearm as he went, and I knew it was on purpose. It was my birthday. He had never gotten close enough to me before that to even remotely be in the vicinity of being able to touch me. But that day he was, and he did.

I felt it all in that moment. The years of built-up tension that twisted my gut into a giant knot of nerves and need, all came undone in that brush of his fingers.

I was never the same.

I haven't been the same.

Every time he saw me from that day forward, his dark eyes burned my skin like he was trying to tell me something without words.

There have only been a handful of other times when he's touched me in the smallest of ways over the years, but every time he does, all I've wished for is to know what it would be like to have his touch everywhere.

The closest I've gotten was a few months ago on my twenty-second birthday. He placed his entire hand on my lower back, guiding me out of the VIP section of the club that's in the casino my family owns in Atlantic City. I had a few drinks already, but his touch made me instantly drunk. His hand singed me, and I felt the need he had for more radiating into and spreading through me.

And then today...

Today he had to go and ask me what was wrong. He read me like an open book, and I hadn't wanted to share the words on my pages as much as I did in that moment.

CHAPTER 4
Katarina

Apparently my brothers don't want to give me any breathing room, because they've suddenly decided it's been too long since our last Sunday family dinner, and tonight is as good as any to put more pressure on me.

I've been cooking all day with my mom, and to my surprise, she hasn't asked me a single question about my meeting in the city yesterday. I was able to avoid her when I got home after driving around aimlessly with Jimmy, but thought for sure I'd get an earful from my her today about family obligations and blah, blah, blah.

But she hasn't said a word. About anything.

Maybe she doesn't know?

I put the garlic bread in the oven and turn to face her, her back still to me as she adds tomatoes to the salad. "So, mom, you know I went into the city yesterday…"

"Mm-hmm. Did you go shopping?"

"Uh, no, I didn't. Leo asked me to go and see him, Alec, and Luca."

She stills at my words, turning around slowly. "What did they want?" she asks, her voice strained.

"They wanted to inform me of a meeting they had on Friday with the Antonuccis. About me." Her face turns to stone — emotionless. "I'll be meeting Santino Antonucci on Saturday."

My mother doesn't say a word, but her eyes hold mine, their honey color so similar to my own. It's in them that I see the sadness she feels, knowing that my fate is the same as hers was. She was a Melcciona before marrying my father and becoming a Carfano, and I don't know that part of my family. I asked my mom about them once, and she said she served her purpose to her family. They received the protection of the Carfanos in exchange for her family's dock properties.

Her value as a human being could literally be measured and set with a price tag.

She must've felt beyond betrayed, because that's how I'm feeling right now. After she married my father, she had no reason to go back to her family aside from weddings and funerals, and she always attended those with my father. Alone. Her family basically wrote her off, and that's what I fear will happen to me.

"I only have one piece of advice for you, Katarina," my mother begins, her eyes boring into mine to make sure I'm listening. "Do what you need to do in order to survive. You're stronger than you know and can find happiness, no matter how small, in the life you will build with him."

And with that, she wipes her hands on a tea towel and walks out of the kitchen, leaving me standing there — stunned.

So that's how she survived. She found what little comfort she could in this house. She was always cooking and cleaning and keeping busy somehow. The fact that she only had those things as reprieves from the life she was dealt, makes me sad. She still only has that, even now that my father has been gone for five years. She's still stuck. She's still hiding. She's still living a life not in her control.

I don't want that life.

I refuse.

Everyone should be arriving within the hour, so I take a deep breath and place the various dishes we made inside the two ovens to keep warm, and head upstairs to take a quick shower.

Shopping has been the only real form of freedom and joy I've gotten outside of this house, and it's kind of all my brothers think I'm good for. So when an idea hits me, I decide I might as well use my love of fashion to my advantage.

Running my hands over all my dresses in my closet, I smile and stop when my fingers brush over the pink velvet of a dress I picked up last winter at a little boutique in the city.

This is the perfect one to accomplish what I'm going to do later. The dusty rose, long-sleeved velvet dress hugs my chest and waist, then flares out slightly from my hips and hits me mid-thigh.

I feel so beautiful in it and it shows off my body in the exact way I want it to. Classy and covered, and yet on full display. I can't wait to feel Dante's eyes on me. For family dinners, I usually just wear a simple dress or jeans or a skirt with a blouse, but tonight requires a little more effort.

Dante has come to fewer and fewer family dinners over the past couple years, but I have a feeling he'll be here tonight, and I'm sure as hell not wasting the opportunity.

Pulling my hair from my bun, I curl it and then apply my makeup, keeping it casual. The dress will speak for itself. I spritz myself with my favorite floral perfume and slip into a pair of nude strappy heels, giving myself a once-over in the mirror.

It's now or never, Kat.

For the first time in a long time, excitement courses through me at the thought of my plan working. Of actually, *finally*, knowing what it feels like to be kissed by a man. Not a peck on the lips from a boy in high school who was too scared to try anything because my brothers had eyes everywhere and it was always known that I was off-limits.

I may not have even really liked him or anyone in high school for it to matter, but that didn't mean I didn't want to know what it would feel like to be kissed.

The sad part is that I felt nothing. Just lips on mine. I want to feel *something* for once, and I know Dante would, without a doubt, make me feel everything and then some.

Checking the time, I see it's almost six, and I head downstairs and right into the kitchen to take everything out of the ovens.

"We thought we'd find you in here."

I turn to see Tessa and Abrianna, Alec and Leo's women, and I smile, placing the dish of baked ziti down on the counter. "Hi, guys."

"Damn, girl, you look good," Abri praises, and I laugh.

"Thanks. I felt like dressing up a little to make myself feel good. And you two look flawless as always," I add, and they both smile their appreciation.

"Do you need any help?" Tessa asks as I take out another dish.

"Yes, thank you. If you don't mind getting out the salad dressings and butter for the table, and then helping me carry everything out into the dining room."

"Sure, of course."

"Is everyone here?"

"For the most part," Abrianna says. "Luca and Angela will be here soon. They left maybe ten minutes after us. How are you, though? Why do you need to make yourself feel good tonight?"

"Oh, uhm…" I shrug, opening the other oven to take out another dish.

"You know you can always call or text us, right?" Tessa tells me.

"Seriously, it can't be easy being alone here in this big house with just your mom," Abri adds, lowering her voice to make sure my mother doesn't hear her. "If you need girl time, we're here for you."

I smile softly. "Thank you. That means a lot. Seriously."

"Of course. Now, what's going on?"

"I don't want you to talk to my brothers because I plan

on handling this in my own way."

"Okay…" Abri says expectantly, her eyes turning fierce, already preparing for the worst.

"I met with all three of them yesterday, and on Saturday, I have a meeting with Santino Antonucci."

"Why?"

"Uhm…" I draw out, "because he will be my husband?"

Tessa's eyes widen. "What?"

"Mm-hmm." I nod, tucking a strand of hair behind my ear.

"Are you serious?"

"I unfortunately am."

"No." Abrianna shakes her head, huffing out a laugh of disbelief. "Leo can't be serious."

"He is. My father told me a long time ago that it was how we did things in our family. As his only daughter, it was especially important for me to know my role. Maybe if I had a sister, or sisters, then I would have some kind of choice in the matter."

"We're fucking Carfanos. What does this other family have that we can't just get ourselves? I have to talk to Leo about this. I have ways of making him listen, you know." She smirks, and I love that she's already referring to herself as a Carfano.

"I don't want to cause problems," I tell her. "I know they made this dinner happen on such short notice to make sure I know how serious they are, but I can handle my brothers. I have a plan. Sort of."

"Just know we're here if you need us. I don't want to lose you when we're only just getting to know each other."

Abrianna and Tessa both hug me and I blink away the urge to cry. I've never known what it was like to have sisters, but with them, I feel the bond already and I don't want to lose that.

My aunt Teresa, Francesca, Maria, and Christina all walk into the kitchen and I clear my throat, plastering a smile on my face. "Hi."

"We're here to help."

"Thanks. Just grab anything."

Walking out of the kitchen and into the dining room, I know Dante's there before I even look around. I can feel his eyes on me.

I'm looking down at the loaves of garlic bread in my hands, then look up to meet his dark gaze. His jaw is set and his fists are clenched on the table as his eyes roam up and down my body before meeting mine again.

I can't read them clearly.

They're heated. They're angry. They're…I don't know…something.

I don't let my steps falter though, and wanting tonight to go as planned, I walk around the table towards him, his eyes following me the entire time.

My brothers are on the other side of the room talking to my uncles in a little group, sipping their drinks, their attention not on Dante or me.

I set the bread down right beside him and his right hand unclenches to rub his jaw. "What are you wearing?" he asks, low and rough so no one else hears.

I turn my back to the table and room and look down at him. "A dress. Is there something wrong with it?" My voice

26

comes out shaky and I hate it.

"You're dressed like you're looking to start something, Katarina. And trust me, you don't want that."

"Maybe I do," I whisper, feeling bold.

Walking back around him, I wait until I'm almost past him to run my finger down the side of his arm so no one else in the room sees me.

He stiffens beneath my touch. I know he wasn't expecting me to touch him. No one touches him. For all the years I've known him and have seen him around other people, they've all kept their distance from him.

Then again, who's crazy enough to touch death when they have a choice?

CHAPTER 5
Dante

This dinner is fucking torture.

I've tortured many people in my life, and I can say without hesitation that I would rather be doing that right now than sitting through a dinner while in the same room as Katarina when she's dressed like that and I can't touch her.

She looks so fucking good. She's always beautiful, but this is beyond that. It's effortless for her. She knows she's gorgeous, but I don't think she realizes just how much.

The dress clings to her tits, hugs her stomach, and then drapes down over her hips, showing off her long legs. It'd be considered modest on anyone else, but on her, it should be fucking illegal for her to wear it.

The softness of the fabric is begging me to run my hands all over it and to feel the body of the goddess beneath. And for that, I know I'd catch a bullet by any of the men at the other end of table. Katarina is off-limits. She's meant for another man. But goddamnit, I don't give a fuck. I haven't for a long fucking time.

And those shoes she's wearing…

Fuck me.

I'd have her keep those heels on so I could feel them dig into my shoulders as I tasted the heaven between her thighs.

Katarina's playing at something tonight, and she's playing with fire. She just struck a match, and if she makes one more fucking move, she's going to light my fuse, and I can't be held responsible for what I do after that.

I've missed a lot of family dinners over the past few years because I can't stand being around her for hours and not have her.

It takes everything in me to not just stare at her the entire time or drag her down the hallway to fuck her until she's screaming my name so everyone here knows who she truly belongs to.

Her father caught on while he was still alive and he brought me into his office, placing his gun on the table to show me he was serious. I remember his exact words like he said them to me five minutes ago.

"I see the way you look at her. I see the way you want her. If you ever try anything with Katarina, I will put a bullet in your skull and no one will ever know you're gone. No one will miss you. I gave you a family. I gave you a chance. I gave you a life in the free world and I gave you a purpose. I saw the potential in you and trained you to be the man

you are today. The goddamn Executioner.

"Do you not enjoy the power you hold over people? They hear your name and they instantly know what they're in for. People fear you. People respect you. People are careful around you. They know not to fuck with you. But let me tell you, people are also the same with me. Don't fuck with me, Dante. Don't fuck with my family. I gave them to you and I can take them away. Are we clear?"

Yes, he was crystal fucking clear, and that kept me in line for a short while. I owed him my loyalty as a debt that was only going to be paid in full with my death. He saved me from prison and a life on the streets, but I couldn't stand not being near her, so I started watching her through the cameras that are mounted around the property. I'd watch and wait for her to go outside so I could catch even a glimpse of her. And every time I did, it calmed me. She has that effect on me. When I still lived in this house, she was the little light that kept me sane.

Tonight though, I'm anything but sane.

My willpower is stretched to the absolute maximum during this dinner. Every time my eyes look down at my plate, I feel hers on me. Everyone's voices become white noise, getting louder with the more wine they drink. They're the family I lost a long time ago, but even so, I've always felt the divide between them and me. I was a part of everything, but still an outsider.

Leo clears his throat and makes eye contact with every man at the table, then stands, which means he wants to have a meeting.

Mrs. Carfano clears her throat. "You can carry your plates to the kitchen on your way," she says to Leo, and he nods.

"Of course, ma."

Her face softens and we all take our plates into the kitchen, stacking them on the counter before continuing on to Michael's old office.

Leo's uncles all took a step back from the business when Leo took over, which allowed him to be who his father wanted him to be, and appointed his own close circle of men to make up his hierarchy. His uncles are still involved in big decisions and are kept up-to-date on everything that goes on, though.

Leo pours himself a drink from the crystal decanter that's on the cart near the bookshelves and then takes a seat behind his father's desk. Everyone follows suit but me. I remain by the door.

The air hangs heavy with the lingering scent of cigars from years past, but with Anthony, Richard, and Carmine all lighting up their cigars, the room fills with a fresh cloud of smoke.

"Alec, Luca, and I met with the Antonuccis on Friday and talked with Katarina yesterday about meeting Santino and Frank this coming Saturday."

"What're they giving us?" Anthony asks.

"We're joining trucking companies with them."

I really don't want to be here, hearing them discuss the gains of marrying off Katarina like she's a fucking commodity.

I've been leaning against the door and no one's eyes have come my way thus far. It's my job to blend in and be invisible when needed, which makes it that much easier for me to slip out without anyone noticing.

I hear the faint clinking of heels down the hall and my head whips around to find Katarina walking towards the bathroom that's a few doors down. Right before she steps in, she looks over her shoulder at me, a small smile gracing her lips when she finds me watching her.

My girl wants to play games, but she has no idea I've been playing this game with her long before tonight. Stalking down the hall quietly, I duck into the shadows of the doorway of the room right across from the bathroom and wait for her.

She steps out a few minutes later and looks left and right, her beautiful face falling when she doesn't see me.

"You looking for me, babygirl?" I ask, stepping out from my hiding spot. "What game are you playing tonight, Katarina?"

"I'm not playing anything," she says softly, her eyes wide.

"I know you better than you think," I challenge. "That dress. Those shoes. You touched me. Are you trying to get my attention?" She looks up at me, her eyes not holding the fear everyone else's does when they look at me. They hold everything that she never lets anyone see. "Because you got my attention." I take a step closer to her. "You've always had my attention. But you already know that, don't you?"

She swallows hard, her throat bobbing along her long, slender neck that I know my hand would fit around with ease to hold her in place while I fuck her.

I step closer to her and she flattens herself against the wall. I reach out and run a single finger up the length of her arm and she shivers, the fabric of her dress doing nothing to hide her reaction to me. I stop at her shoulder before I reach her bare skin, knowing that if I touch her, that'll be the end of the both of us.

"You're testing all of my patience tonight, Katarina." I want to hold back, and I know I should, but I'm already going to hell and she's already promised to another man, so I might as well give in to what we both want.

I let my finger slide over the edge of her dress to touch her bare skin, and her mouth pops open on a sigh. She licks her lips, the tip of her pretty pink tongue peeking out to moisten the lips I want to taste.

My cock jumps at the sight, wanting to feel that tip rimming me before she takes me into her hot mouth. It's a sight I've pictured for years, and have beaten my cock raw to so many times I've lost count.

Her pupils dilate, the honey-brown almost obliterated by their black centers. I knew my Katarina would react like this. I've waited years for this moment.

I spread my hand over the center of her chest and slide it up her throat just in time to feel her sharp intake of breath. She swallows, her chest rising and falling with quick breaths, but her eyes still not showing an ounce of fear. They're filled with desire. She wants this as much as I do.

I've dreamt of feeling her pulse beneath my touch and I can feel it now, beating so fast it pounds into my hand like a fucking drum. I'm feeling her life in my hands.

Katarina's pure. She's innocent despite this little show she's putting on tonight, and I've waited years to dirty her up. I've waited years to take my beautiful Katarina, as unadulterated as freshly fallen snow, and see her melt into a puddle beneath me.

I take another step closer, still not touching her anywhere other than my hand around her throat, and there's just a fraction of space separating us now.

Her pulse jumps and I stare down at her. "You like playing with fire? Your brothers are right down the hall. Your whole family is. What do you think they'd do if they saw me this close to you? My hand wrapped around your throat? Do you think they'd wait long enough to see that you like it before they cut my hand off for touching you? Do you think they'd kill me on the spot?"

Her breath hitches.

And when she scrapes her teeth across her bottom lip, it's my fucking undoing.

Growling, I pull her away from the wall by the throat and wrap my other arm around her waist, dragging her into the room across the hall where I was hiding before. Lifting her up, I pin her against the wall with my knee between her legs to hold her up.

Sliding my thumb up and down the column of her throat, I drag my nose across her jaw and her breathing becomes erratic. "I can feel your hot little cunt against my knee. Are you wet for me, Katarina?" I whisper roughly in her ear, and when she doesn't respond, I tap the side of her throat. "Answer me," I demand.

"Yes," she sighs.

"I know no one's ever touched you before, babygirl. Your brothers saw to that. *I saw to that.*"

Her hips start to rock against my knee, and it takes every

ounce of strength I have not to tear whatever she has on beneath that dress off and feel how fucking wet she is for me.

"That's it," I rasp in her ear. "Take what you want from me. I want to be the first man to make you come. And when you meet that little prick your brothers want you to marry on Saturday, I want you to think of this moment right now. I want you to see if you feel like this around him. If he'll make you want to ride his leg like a fucking horse." Katarina squeaks out a little moan and her hips move faster. "You're going to have to be quiet, babygirl, or your family will hear you."

Her hands reach out to grip my suit jacket as she keeps sliding her hot pussy all over my leg. I'm never washing these goddamn pants again.

"I want to feel you come on me, Katarina. Give me a piece of you that no other man will ever have." She begins to shake, and her little mewls of pleasure turn to moans despite how hard I know she's trying to hold back.

"I said be quiet," I growl in her ear, and I feel her jaw clench against my cheek, doing as I say. I lick the shell of her ear and she shudders. "Good girl. I know you're close, Katarina."

"Kiss me," she whispers, her voice barely audible.

"What was that?"

"Kiss me. Please," she begs, pressing herself harder against me as she grinds unabashedly, using me for her pleasure.

"Fuck," I grunt, lifting my leg higher on wall, taking more of her weight. "I'll take that first from you, too."

I slam my mouth down on hers and she moans on

impact, her hips rocking faster against me. I groan, licking the seam of her lips, demanding entrance so I can take everything from her that I've wanted to take from her without mercy.

She's mine.

She's always been mine.

I sweep my tongue into her mouth and she meets mine tentatively, like she's afraid. I know she doesn't know what to do, but I'll teach her.

Katarina moans, and my fingers put pressure on her throat. I'm nowhere near constricting her airway or hurting her, though. I could never hurt her.

I know she's close with how hard she's shaking, so I bite down on her lip and suck it into my mouth, giving her what I know she needs. She moans louder, and I capture her lips again to swallow her sounds as I feel her hot come drenching my leg.

Fuck. Me.

Stepping back, I release her and she stumbles, reaching out to steady herself on the first thing she finds in the dark.

If I don't stop now, then I'll end up fucking her until she's raw. Then I really will have taken all of her firsts in the span of minutes with her family right down the hall. And there's no way I could make her be silent while I'm deep inside of her. They'd all know, and I'd be dead before I got more than just a taste of heaven.

Sucking in a deep breath to calm myself before I walk back out there, I leave her with one last thing. "Tonight, when you're lying in bed, I want you to touch that pretty little pussy of yours and try to make yourself feel as good as you do right now. You'll find out you can't."

Adjusting my suit jacket, I steel my face and walk out of there like I didn't just have the only future worth having in my grip, and like I don't have the darling princess's come soaking my pant leg from being under the touch of a man who's nowhere near worthy of having her.

CHAPTER 6
Katarina

Dante disappears and I slide down the wall until I hit the floor, physically unable to support myself. My head is spinning and my legs are Jell-o. I feel boneless, dizzy, and my heart is racing so fast, I can't believe it hasn't burst yet.

Sucking in breath after breath through my tight lungs, I pinch my eyes closed, and a few tears escape.

I just experienced the most intense pleasure of my life with a man who I've dreamt of having touch me for years.

Did that really just happen?

I don't know how long I sit here, my mind blank while simultaneously running a marathon of its own, barely able to process what just happened.

I don't even know what room I'm in. I never go down the hallway where my father's office is. I was never allowed to when he was still alive, and I've had no reason to after he died, but I wanted Dante to know I was out here. And somehow, he knew.

When I feel I can trust my legs again, I untie my heels and roll onto my knees, gripping the doorframe to stand. Dante didn't even touch me aside from his hand around my throat and on my waist, and yet my entire body feels destroyed. I can't even imagine what it would feel like to have him touch every inch of me.

The light coming from underneath the door of my father's office lets me know my brothers and uncles are still in there, and I quickly make my way down the hall, holding my heels close to my chest. I take a roundabout way to the staircase so no one sees me, and go straight up to my room.

Collapsing on top of my bed, my shoes hit the carpet with a dull thud as I stare at the ceiling. My hand drifts up to my neck to feel my throat, and my breath hitches. Having his hand over my throat was the sexiest thing and something I had no idea I'd like. Having his big, strong hand there didn't feel like he wanted to hurt me, but rather was his version of a caress.

My God, I want to feel that again.

And his voice…

I've never heard him talk so much, and everything he said was so dirty and so damn hot.

Rubbing my thighs together, I feel myself getting slick again, and just like he wanted me to do, I lift the skirt of my dress and pull my already soaked panties to the side, replaying everything that happened earlier in my head.

My clit is throbbing, begging for attention. I want Dante, but my own fingers will have to do.

I start with slow circles, then pick up speed when I picture his hand around my throat, feeling how fast my heart is beating for him.

I'm still sensitive, so it doesn't take long for my legs to start shaking. I bite my lip, feeling his teeth on the same spot, his tongue against mine, and his groan vibrating through me.

My throat closes at the memory and I throw my arm over my face to muffle the moans I can't hold back as I come for the second time tonight. It's nowhere near what I felt with him, but it's enough to take the edge off.

I already know that nothing short of Dante will do from now on.

Shimmying out of my panties, I lift my dress over my head and toss them both to the floor. I slide beneath the covers as tears gather in my eyes from both anger and sadness. I just don't know which one is winning.

CHAPTER 7
Katarina

This week has gone by slow, and yet quicker than I wanted. Every thought has been filled with Dante and me in that room, and how I wish there could have been more. But what I want hasn't stopped today from coming.

Today's the day I meet the Antonuccis and the man my brothers want to marry me off to.

What do you wear when you want to make an impression with a man you don't want to make an impression on, but you have to anyway?

I decide to go with a light blue dress and pair it with a navy blue blazer and pumps.

I curl my hair and pull the top part back into a bun on

top of my head and then apply my makeup and add jewelry, forcing a smile in the mirror when I'm done to test it out like I always do.

Checking my phone, I see it's time to go, and I head downstairs, finding my brothers already waiting for me. All three of them look at my outfit and nod, giving me their silent approval, and I hate them for it. I feel like a show pony about to be walked around for judgement and rating to see if I'm good enough. Why does it have to be me that's good enough? Why isn't it if he's good enough for me?

I silently follow them outside. I have nothing to say. But when I spot Dante leaning against the lead Range Rover beside Jimmy, my steps falter and I almost stumble down the front stairs. He immediately pushes off the car and takes a few steps forward, ready to catch me, but I steady myself on my own. He looks me up and down, his normally emotionless face revealing a pinch of both concern and anger.

"I'm riding with Dante," I announce, and my brothers turn around to look at me. "Alone. I can't be in a car with any of you right now."

Their eyebrows pull together in confusion and Leo rubs his jaw, looking over at Dante and then me, giving a small nod.

With the three of them walking off to the other Range Rover, I breathe a sigh of relief and look back to Dante. I can see that he already knows I wanted to be alone with him, and he opens the back door for me.

I climb up inside and he slides in next to me. The second the door closes, I can hear the beating of my heart pounding in my ears and I'm hyper aware of him next to me. He's calm, he's still, and when I peek up at his face, it's unreadable.

He looks over at me and my eyes dart back down to my lap, twisting and fiddling with my fingers.

"Jimmy, I have to talk to Katarina about what's about to happen," Dante tells him, and Jimmy gives a curt nod.

Dante presses the button to raise the partition my brothers had custom made and installed in all of their cars for privacy. The second it's fully raised, Dante rubs his jaw — a move I've only seen him make around me. I think he's trying not to touch me, even though that's exactly what I want him to do.

"I'm not leaving your side today, Katarina," he says roughly. "No matter what is said, you're not going to show any fear, annoyance, or hatred. You're going to wear that mask that you always wear, and you're not going to let any of them see past it. Do you understand?"

I give him a nod, but he says, "No. Tell me you understand."

"I understand."

"Good."

"But I am…" I trail off, rolling my lips between my teeth.

"You're what?"

"I am a little afraid. I know this is important for my brothers and for the family, but I don't want this."

Dante's face turns to stone and his eyes harden to granite. It's that same look from outside the elevator last week that he slips in and out of. "As long as I'm there, you don't have to be afraid. They're all afraid of me. I'll protect you."

My heart swells momentarily at his words, but then deflates just as fast because they're just words. I know he can protect me from danger, but he can't protect me from what's about to happen. I wish he could. I wish he could just take me away and I wish I didn't feel so obligated to my family the way I do, but I am. I love my brothers. I just wish they loved me a little more to see what they're doing to me.

I don't say anything else to Dante. I turn my head away and look out the window. A few minutes pass in strained silence before his rough voice sends a chill down my spine. "Did you do as I said?"

I know he wants to know if I touched myself on Sunday, and because I have absolutely nothing to lose, I turn back to look him in the eyes when I admit, "Yes. Every single night." His nostrils flare as he sucks in a sharp breath. "But it wasn't the same."

"Did you use your fingers?"

"Yes."

"And you wished they were mine?"

"Yes," I sigh, feeling my face flush as my hands grip the hem of my dress.

"If I slid my hand under your dress right now, what would I find? Would I find you wet for me?"

Biting my lip, I nod. "Please," I find myself begging.

"Please, what?" he counters, tilting his head to the side.

"Please touch me."

"You want me to touch you? You want me to make you come all over my hand right before you meet the man you're supposed to marry?"

"Yes," I practically moan, and Dante reaches out to grip my leg above my knee, sliding me towards him.

"Come here." He taps his leg and takes my hand to help me as I throw my leg over the both of his, straddling his lap.

His hands slide up my thighs and under the skirt of my dress to my hips. Hooking a single finger beneath the waistband of my panties, he slides it across my lower abdomen, my legs automatically squeezing around his, desperate to know his touch.

I lean back against the partition and Dante snaps the elastic band against my skin, running his knuckle down the wet seam of my pussy, the lace already clinging to me.

"This is all for me," he growls, pressing his knuckle against my clit. I bite my lip and moan. "The partition might be soundproof to us talking, but it won't be if you get any louder. Can you be quiet for me again?"

I nod frantically, and he rewards me with a swirl of his knuckle around my tight bundle of nerves, making me whimper and fall forward, my hands gripping his shoulders.

"Good girl," he praises.

Pulling my panties to the side, Dante runs his knuckle down my bare seam this time, and I almost orgasm from that alone. We groan together.

"Fuck," he grunts. "You're so hot and wet for me, babygirl." His finger slides down to swirl my entrance and my muscles contract automatically, needing him inside of me.

His other hand comes to grip my chin and he lifts my head to look him in the eyes. "Before I fuck you with my fingers, I need to know if anything has ever been inside of you before." I shake my head no, and his grip on my chin tightens. "Not even your own fingers? A vibrator?"

I shake my head again and his teeth gnash together, his eyes pinching closed for a moment. Whenever I needed to, I would just get myself off by rubbing my clit.

"I'm taking another of your firsts, babygirl. You think your husband's going to like that?"

"He's not my husband. And I want it to be you."

Pulling my face to his, Dante kisses me hard, his lips fusing to mine as he slides his hand to the back of my head, deepening the kiss.

His tongue tangles with mine before he pulls back. "Good answer," he rasps just as he pushes his finger inside of me.

A deep moan is ripped from me as I feel something greater than I've ever known. My inner muscles squeeze him tightly, not used to the intrusion as he rubs my clit with his thumb.

"Look at me," he demands, and my eyes find his. Spreading his knees apart, mine spread with him, opening me wider so he can add a second finger. I bite down on my lip to hold in my moans, but it's no use.

"Dante," I moan, and his black eyes burn into mine.

His fingers are inside of me, thick and rough as he stretches me open, sliding in and out of me. I choke out a cry. It hurts at the same time it sends sparks of pleasure through me.

"Dante," I moan again, my whole body shaking from the pressure that's quickly rising in me.

Twisting the two fingers he has inside of me, Dante curls them inward at the same time he presses down on my clit, and I lose it, collapsing against his chest. My face buried in his neck muffles my groans while his fingers continue to move slowly in and out and he rubs small circles around my sensitive clit, sending aftershocks through me that has me coming until I'm completely empty.

Somewhere in the haze, I realize how much of me is touching him, and I pull back to look at him, gaging his reaction. All I see is heat.

Dante slips his fingers out of me and brings them to his lips, licking them clean. Humming, he keeps his eyes on me. "You taste how you look," he murmurs.

"And how's that?"

"Like purity and sin wrapped together."

The car slows to a stop and Jimmy knocks on the partition, snapping me back to reality. I climb off Dante's lap and try to smooth my dress back into place.

Reaching into my purse by my feet, I pull out a compact mirror and check to make sure I still look presentable. I glide on a layer of nude lipstick and run my fingers through my hair, all the while feeling Dante's eyes on me, watching my every move.

"Remember what I said before," he says, turning my face so I'll look at him again. "If you get caught up in your head, just know I'm standing behind you, my fingers stained with your come. I know that's what's going to be on my mind when I have to hold back from killing that fucker."

"Why would you want to kill him?"

"For taking what's mine," he says, then opens the door before I can say anything.

Dante holds the door open for me, and when my heels

hit the pavement, his eyes scan me from my feet to my face. He just said I'm his, and God help me, because I want to be his more than anything. And God help me even more, because I wouldn't mind if he killed Santino to have me.

Alec, Leo, and Luca walk up to us before Dante or I can say anything more, and Dante turns, leading us into Giorgio's. I follow behind my brothers, with Jimmy beside me and Alfie behind all of us.

Once inside, I see two tables set up for lunch. A long rectangular one and a square one set for two.

"Katarina, that's your table," Leo tells me, pointing at the two-top. "You're going to eat with Santino."

I don't say a single word.

I didn't know I was going to be put on the spot for an entire meal, sitting across from this guy and talking to him while everyone looks on.

This is so messed up.

Eyeing the table, I take a deep breath. "I need a minute. I'll be right back," I announce, turning towards the back hallway where I know the bathrooms are. Leo steps in front of me before I even make it three steps.

"Don't even think about running. We learned our lesson from Angela and have every exit covered."

"I wasn't going to run," I all but sneer, and step around him. I don't know what he's talking about, but if Angela came here for a fucked-up meeting like this and was able to run, then good for her. I like her even more now.

I close and lock the bathroom door when I get inside and pace the small area. My dress suddenly feels too tight, my heels are pinching my feet, and my skin is burning.

I have to take deliberate breaths to calm myself down.

I can do this.

I'm a Carfano. I'm built different. I can handle this.

The one thing that has the ability to derail my confidence, though, is the fact that the same man who just had his fingers inside of me will be sitting ten feet away while I talk to my supposed future husband.

And while the thought of Dante's fingers inside of me momentarily calms me, my already soaking wet panties get even wetter. They're far too distracting, and they're far too much of a reminder of what just happened to wear them for an entire meal.

Shimmying them off, I ball them in my fist to stuff them in my purse just as a knock raps against the door.

I let out a frustrated breath. "I said I needed a minute."

"They're here," I hear Dante say. "It's time."

Taking another deep breath, I look at myself in the mirror and wait for all of my emotions to fall away.

Everything I want doesn't matter.

Everything I've been told doesn't matter.

Nothing matters but clearing my head.

When my mask slips into place, I pull my shoulders back and open the door. Dante looks me up and down, his eyes swirling around my face. Satisfied with what he sees, he gives me a small nod and steps back. But it's not that easy, and a surge of anger courses through me.

I take a step towards him and slap my balled-up panties to his chest. "I can't sit through a meal with *him* while wearing these, and it's your fault."

Narrowing his eyes, his hand covers mine and he takes

the wet lace from my grip, bringing it right to his nose to inhale my scent before slipping the fabric into the inner breast pocket of his suit jacket.

His eyes flare, but he doesn't say anything. He just steps to the side and I walk past him, feeling his eyes travel down the length of me from behind. And knowing I'm not wearing any panties, a slow, genuine smile curls my lips up. It's another secret kept between only Dante and me.

Walking tall with my head held high, I round the corner into the main seating area, and all the men in the room stand. It's the act of gentlemen, but I don't see a gentleman in sight. Every single one of them has blood on their hands that can't be washed off. They take what they want, with or without permission, and give zero apologies for it.

I come from a long line of men just like them, which means I can be just like them. I can channel that same energy.

Smiling at each and every one of them, including my brothers, I walk over to Frank Antonucci and hold my hand out. "Hello, Mr. Antonucci, I'm Katarina."

"Please, call me Frank. It's so lovely to meet you, Katarina. This is my son, Santino." He lets go of my hand and I hold mine out to his son. He takes it and brings it to his mouth, kissing my knuckles. His warm lips on my skin doesn't make my whole arm tingle like a simple touch from Dante does, though.

"Katarina Carfano, it's nice to finally meet you. You're even more beautiful than I was told."

His compliment does nothing for me, but I give him my best smile anyway. "That's so nice of you to say. Thank you."

"It's the truth," he says simply, a glint in his eyes that I hate. He's looking at me like I'm just a pretty thing being handed to him on a silver platter. He thinks I'm a forgone conclusion. Which to be fair, I'm supposed to be, but not if I can help it.

I can feel Dante's eyes more than anyone's burning into me from behind and I do my best to ignore him. To ignore all of them.

Walking around the table, Santino pulls the chair out for me and I sit, immediately crossing my legs under the table. I place my napkin on my lap and take a sip of water, brutally aware of how naked I am under my dress.

"So, Katarina, what do you like to do for fun?" Santino asks casually to break the silence.

"Fun," I say on a small laugh, holding back from rolling my eyes. "I don't know about fun, but I like to cook and bake. I read a little. Shop." I lift one shoulder in a small shrug. "And when I'm really feeling crazy, I like to go to my family's casino in Atlantic City and try my luck at the tables."

I know I shocked him with that last one, because his eyes widen and he laughs. "What's your poison?"

"Poker. I tend to be underestimated, and I've been told I have a great poker face."

He grins. "You just have a great face."

"Thank you." I feel my cheeks heat slightly and I don't know why. I'm certainly not flirting with him even though I know he is with me. I guess I just don't get many chances to be complimented.

I've never been allowed to date, but even if I was, my brothers would certainly scare off anyone who showed interest. They even scared the girls away while I was in school, which meant I never had any true friends, just classroom acquaintances.

Even now when I leave the house, I'm always with Jimmy. I've managed to slip away from him a few times to go driving around by myself, but I've always either just returned on my own without truly going anywhere, or have been found and brought home before I get the chance to do anything or go anywhere.

"What do you do for fun, Santino? Or is it a I'm-not-allowed-to-know kind of thing?" My guess is that he likes to indulge in women and gambling. He gives off a confident vibe while also holding back.

"It's part that." He smirks. "But I wouldn't mind taking you in a card game." I knew it.

"Sounds fun." It really doesn't, but I return his smirk and rip off a piece of bread from the basket between us. I dip it in the seasoned oil on the table and his eyes follow my mouth as I chew and swallow. "But don't say I didn't warn you. I may just take all of your money."

He smiles wide and leans forward on the table. "Well, as you already know, soon what's mine will be yours. So, I'll take that challenge." He winks and leans back casually, taking a sip of wine.

My stomach knots at his casual remark, and we spend the rest of lunch making small talk about nothing in particular or of meaning. That marriage joke fortified my walls, and I didn't reveal anything else of importance about myself.

Finally, after what seems like hours, Leo clears his throat and stands, shaking Frank's hand. "We'll talk soon," Leo tells him assuredly.

Frank comes over to our table, and knowing how this game of power works, I don't stand. I dab the corners of my mouth with my napkin and hold my hand out for him to take.

Frank gives me a small bow of his shoulders. "It was very nice to meet you, Katarina."

"You as well." I smile, and Santino stands, taking my hand next.

"Thank you for the lovely company, Katarina. I hope to talk to you soon." He places a card down on the table beside my plate. "If you want to talk or need anything."

I can feel Dante's anger seeping out of him, permeating the air as it leaves his body, but I give Santino a smile and a small nod by way of agreeing without having to say the words aloud. I don't want to lie to him, because there's no way I'm going to willingly call this man to talk or for anything else, but I politely tuck the card into my purse since everyone is watching our exchange.

The second Frank and Santino leave though, I throw my napkin on the table and stand. I walk the length of the dining area and run my hand through my hair. I watch the people walking by on the sidewalk through the large front window for a few seconds before turning back to find everyone in the room staring at me.

I open my mouth to say something to all of them, but the moment I gather my thoughts and take a step towards them, the sharp piercing sound of glass breaking has me freezing on the spot.

It's like time is warped. I can only hear the dull shouts of everyone over the thumping of my pulse. My eyes find Dante's across the room and his face is thunderously mad as he shouts, running straight for me. It isn't until I feel fire rip through my leg that the world becomes loud again.

I scream and fall to my knees, gunshots continuing to fire until the entire glass window shatters around me and Dante tackles me, his arms taking the brunt of the fall as we roll through the glass. My head hits the hardwood floor and pain shoots up through me from my leg.

I let out a whimper and Dante's arms tighten around me. "I've got you," he rasps in my ear. "I've got you," he repeats, and I let his words swim around in my head, knowing their truth.

His body on top of mine is the ultimate blanket of protection, and when the bullets stop, the only thing I can hear through the pounding of my pulse are the shouts of men and the crunching of boots on glass as the place is flooded with my family's men.

Dante lifts his head to them. "Bring the cars around to the back alley and get Leo and them out of here! NOW! I've got Katarina!"

He waits a few seconds until the men move away from us and then he's hauling me up with him. I go to put weight on my left leg and whimper in pain again.

Squatting down in front of me, Dante examines my leg. "Fuck," he curses under his breath. "A bullet grazed you and there's glass in the wound."

Panic courses through me. "What?"

"I've got you, babygirl," he assures me, lifting me up into his arms.

"You better make sure my dress is covering me," I whisper to him, and his eyes shoot down to mine.

"I would never let anyone see what's mine," he says, and I feel a pang in my chest at hearing him call me his again. Not in pain, but in…something else. I'm not his. But that doesn't stop me from liking the sound of it.

Dante runs through the dining area and kitchen and out the back door that leads to an alley where Jimmy already has the back door open for us. He places me up inside while the first SUV speeds off into traffic. He climbs in next to me and immediately reaches for me, bringing me back to him to cradle me on his lap.

"Go! Go! Go!" Dante yells at Jimmy, pounding on the back of the passenger's seat. Taking his phone out, Dante dials a number. "Meet us in the medical suite. We're on our way and will be there within twenty minutes."

Hanging up, he dials another number straight away, and I can hear Leo's loud voice ask, "How is she?"

Dante's eyes are on me when he answers, "She was grazed by one of the bullets. I've already called the doctor so he'll be waiting for us when we arrive."

"Bring her up there and then meet us in the conference room," Leo clips, and Dante silently slips his phone back in his pocket without saying another word, wrapping his arm around me again.

"You're going to be okay," he tells me, his eyes boring into mine.

"What about you? Are you okay?"

"I'm okay as long as you're okay," he answers, and my heart flutters in my chest.

Feeling brave, I reach up and glide my finger over the scar that runs down the right side of his face and jaw. I wish I knew the story behind it. Our eyes are locked, and his penetrate mine, trying to read my mind.

He's the only thing keeping me from feeling the pain in my leg right now. He takes my mind off of everything. Off of the shitty lunch I just had to endure, and about everything that happens next.

We pull into the underground garage of my family's building and I wince from being jostled, which has Dante's arms automatically tightening around me.

Jimmy races to the elevators and then slams on the brakes, hopping out to open the back door for us. Placing me down on the seat, Dante climbs out first and then reaches back in for me.

He punches in the code to the elevator, balancing me on his leg with one arm while he presses his finger to the fingerprint pad and puts his eye near the retina scanner. Once he's accepted, he pushes the button marked MD for the medical suite, which is the floor right below the penthouse, and is outfitted with almost everything one would find in a hospital.

We shoot up the building, finding the doctor waiting for us when we step off the elevator. I keep my eyes on Dante's mouth as it moves, explaining everything that happened.

We're led down the hall and into an exam room where Dante gently places me down on a hospital bed and takes my heels off, placing them and my purse on the chair beside me.

I've been pretty numb to the pain thus far, especially when I had Dante's arms around me to distract me, but I can feel it all now.

I look down to watch the doctor examine the area, and I start to feel dizzy.

That's my leg?

My entire left calf is covered in blood.

Groaning, I pinch my eyes closed so I don't have to see it anymore and clamp my mouth shut to hold in the pain.

"You better take good fucking care of her," Dante threatens, and I open my eyes to see him step up close to the doctor. "Because if anything happens to her, you know what I'll do to you."

"Trust me, I know," the doctor says calmly, continuing his examination of my leg.

Dante looks back at me, and as much as I want to ask him to stay, I know I can't. I heard Leo when he told him to go down and meet him after bringing me up here. They have to figure out what happened today.

"It's okay," I tell him, seeing the battle in his eyes. "I'll be okay."

Nodding, he rubs the back of his neck, and I can tell he wants to say or do something else, but can't while we have an audience. Instead, he just gives me a long look, then leaves me alone with the doctor who promptly injects me with a numbing agent before cleaning the wound of all the small glass shards that got lodged inside. The clinking of glass hitting the metal bowl as he removes them just reminds me of how close I came to dying today.

Dante saved my life.

If he hadn't tackled me to the floor, I know another bullet would have hit me, and I know it wouldn't have just been another graze to my leg.

"You'll have a scar, unfortunately," the doctor informs me as he's stitching me up.

"A scar is the least of my problems." My voice sounds foreign to my ears as I stare up at the ceiling. Tears fall from the corners of my eyes, dripping past my ears and onto the pillow.

I don't care about a scar.

I care about the man who walked out of here, threatening to kill the doctor helping me if anything happened to me.

CHAPTER 8
Dante

The elevator doors slide closed and I slice my fingers through my hair.

FUCK!

She's hurt.

She's hurt and it's my fault. I was just trying to protect her and yet I had her rolling in the fucking glass, making it worse.

Pounding my fist into the metal siding of the elevator car, I leave a small dent and curse when glass I didn't even know I had in me, digs into my skin further.

Fuck.

Examining my hands, I remove the small shards with my

knife and place them in my pocket. I don't need Katarina coming in this elevator later and stepping on them.

My hands are full of so many tiny scars already, these fresh cuts don't even faze me. But the fact that Katarina's beautiful skin will now be forever marked as a reminder of this day makes me fucking seethe with anger.

I wanted to stay with her to make sure the doctor does his damn job right, but I need to find out who did this. Because whoever did, needs to fucking die.

When the elevator doors slide open again, I can hear Leo yelling from here, and when I walk into the conference room, he turns his anger on me, slamming his fist on the glass table. "What the fuck happened? You were supposed to make sure the perimeter was secure."

"It was secure. You know we had the area swept this morning and then monitored the entire time before and during the meeting. They were long-range shots, not from street level."

Leo blows out a rough breath, his jaw clenched. "The only other people who knew we would all be there besides us were the Antonuccis, and I sure as fuck wouldn't shoot at myself. Luca, call them and get them here. Now."

"Got it." Luca pulls his phone out and walks out into the hall.

"Alec, call Tessa and have her, Abri, and Angela go and get Kat and bring her up to my place when the doctor is done with her. They'll keep her calm."

Nodding, Alec follows Luca out of the room with his phone in his hand.

"Stefano, run facial recognition on every street camera

within a five-block radius against our known list of enemies first, then widen for anyone suspicious. And hack into Frank and Santino's phones. Find out who the fuck they've been messaging. I want to know if it was them for sure before they get here."

Stefano is a captain, but he's also the family's hacker and the nerve center for everything we do. His fingers fly across the keys of his laptop with his brows pinched together in determination.

Nico, Marco, and Gabriel, were also called in for this shitstorm. Stefano's brothers, Marco and Gabriel, are also captains for the family, and Nico, for a lack of a better description, is Leo's right-hand-man.

"Fuck, fuck, fuck," Stefano mutters a few minutes later, and Leo comes around to look at his screen.

"What did you find?"

"This past week, since your initial meeting, Frank has been in contact with one number that he's never had contact with before, and I traced it back to the Armenians. Nick's doing cleanup right now at Giorgio's, and he just sent a picture of the bullets he dug out from the wall. He was able to read the headstamp on a few, and they're marked with Armenia's code and made for an AK-103. Armenia's military's rifle of choice."

Fuck. Last month we raided their stash house, shot them up, then blew the place to the ground. That crazy motherfucker, Diran Aleksanyan, had his own warehouse wired with explosives and was going to blow it up with all of us still inside, including himself, but Luca shot and killed him before he could press the button. We did, though, when we cleared out. Easier cleanup for us.

We had a truce in place with the Aleksanyan family that defined our territorial boundaries, but throughout this past year, they began dropping the bodies of their enemies onto our territory, trying to draw attention to us.

Diran and his brother, Hovan, were both leaders of the family, but Hovan wasn't there when we took them all out. He has to be the one behind this.

"How the fuck did they find out it was us? You said there were no cameras," Leo barks.

"There weren't. The entire block was abandoned."

"Well, Frank and Santino will just have to tell us, then. LUCA!" Leo shouts to get his attention out in the hall, and he comes back into the room. "Are they coming?"

"They'll be here in forty minutes. I told Frank if he didn't turn his car around and get here within the hour, then we'd come after his entire family in two."

"Dante, meet them in the lobby and bring them to the basement."

I give him a curt nod and head down to wait for them, my mind on Katarina the entire time. The doctor better have given her something for the pain. I don't want her in pain.

When the Antonucci's car pulls up and Frank and Santino step out, they look up at the building, and the look on Frank's face tells me he already knows his fate while Santino looks mildly amused. *Fucking prick.*

The moment they walk through the door and see me standing there, fear flashes through their eyes. I love that look. Fear is my fuel.

I pat them down for weapons and hand them to our

man behind the front desk. "You can have these back later. Walk," I order with a nod to the elevators, then stick my arm out to stop the man they brought with them. "You stay here."

"That's not fucking happening."

"Sammy, stay here. We'll be fine," Frank tells him.

"Boss…"

"I said, stay here."

The bodyguard's lips press together to stop further argument and he takes a seat in the lobby while I walk Frank and Santino to the elevator. When we get down to the basement, they hesitate to step out.

"Walk."

"What's going on? Why are we here?" Santino asks dumbly.

"The conference room down here has more privacy. Now walk," I bark, and they obey without further question.

The short hallway opens up to our large gym area where we have a full set up, equipped with an MMA cage and a boxing ring on one side, and weights and grappling mats to practice our hand-to-hand combat skills on the other side.

Ahead of us is another hallway that's lined with cells for interrogation, and off down another hallway to the right, past the conference room, is a shooting range with a fully stocked artillery beside it.

"In there," I direct when we're outside the conference room door.

Leo, Luca, Alec, Nico, Gabriel, Marco, and Stefano are all sitting together on one end of the table, with two chairs across from them that Frank and Santino sit in.

"What's this about, Leo?" Frank asks first, eyeing everyone before him. "You call my son and I back, bring us to your basement, and then put us before the firing squad?"

"Who from the Aleksanyan family have you been talking to?" Frank's moment of valor is replaced by guilt and fear that flashes across his face. "Talk. Now."

"Hovan found out it was you who blew up his warehouse and has been following you around, waiting for a weak moment to strike. They saw us meet last week and contacted me."

"So you're the reason Katarina almost died today."

"What? Is she okay?" Santino asks right away. "What the fuck did you do, dad?"

"I did what I had to. He threatened our entire family. You know how insane Diran was? His brother is worse."

Leo takes the bait and leans forward, his face devoid of everything. "So, you decided you were more afraid of him than me, even knowing I'd find out? Or did you assume I'd never find out since the deal was to kill us?" He leans back. "It's interesting how people think they can keep coming for us. Even when we show them what happens when they do, they still try. The Cicariellos, the Chen brothers, the Armenians, and now you."

Santino clears his throat and stands. "Leo, I had nothing to do with what my father had arranged. I would never cross you."

Frank looks up at him in disgust and then back at Leo. "He threatened to have my entire family murdered in front of me before killing me himself. All he wanted was the time and place of our next meeting with you in exchange for not coming after us."

Leo gives me the nod and I pull my gun out and press it to the side of Frank's head, which has Santino clearing his throat.

"Leo," Santino starts. "I had nothing to do with this. My father made the mistake of underestimating you, and I never have or would. I was fully on board, and still am, with bringing our families together."

"Santino, what the fuck are you doing?" his father asks, shocked at his son's betrayal.

"Protecting our family. You clearly didn't do that very well."

"You should've known that Hovan would've killed you anyway," Leo says, then gives me another nod and I pull the trigger, blowing a hole in Frank's head and silencing the bullshit coming from his mouth.

"Santino, I'll be in touch with regards to Katarina," Leo says casually. "And if Hovan contacts you, you'll contact me straight away. Because if I find out that you're trying to cross me, you'll meet the same fate as your father. Understood? Good," he says without waiting for an actual answer. "We'll talk later."

Santino runs his hands down the front of his jacket, buttons it, and then walks out without looking at his father's lifeless body. I tuck my gun into its holster and follow behind him to bring him back up to the lobby.

His body guard stands. "Where's Frank?"

"Let's go."

Hiding his shock, he only hesitates a beat before nodding his allegiance and collecting their guns.

Back in the basement, I find two men carrying off Frank's body while others get to work on cleaning up the mess.

"I'll be tracing Santino's phone to ensure he doesn't make the same mistake Frank did."

"What about Katarina?" I ask. "She's not safe back on Staten Island with the gunman still out there. Neither is your mom"

"I know. Kat's staying here, and I've already started the process of moving our mother to one of our safe houses in Miami for a while. We're going to go check on Kat now," he tells me. "And just a heads up, I'm putting her in the other apartment on your floor. She's clearly not afraid of you anymore, and I trust you to protect her if needed."

Nodding, I head up to my apartment, and when I take my phone from my pocket, I feel the brush of Katarina's panties and pull them out. Inhaling her sweet scent, my cock hardens.

She's so fucking perfect. Even more than I already knew.

Taking my suit jacket and shirt off, I toss them into the bin to be burned later since they have blood spatter and glass on them. My pants, though, I fold over the chair in the corner of my room. They're the ones from Sunday. I wore them as a reminder to myself of what's at stake.

I had her come soaked into my pants and her wet panties in my pocket, and yet she's still off limits to me. What's not off limits to me, though, is putting a bullet in Santino's head before I ever let her marry him, or anyone else.

CHAPTER 9
Katarina

The doctor ties off the thread of my stitches and covers the wound with gauze, taping off the edges.

"Make sure you keep it dry for the next 48 hours."

"Okay. Thank you."

There's a knock at the door and it opens a crack. "Can we come in?" I hear Abrianna ask.

"Yes," I call out, and she, Tessa, and Angela filter inside.

"How are you?" Tessa asks first.

"I'm fine. I was grazed by a bullet and then rolled in glass, but I'll be okay."

"What?" she asks in surprise, and Angela's eyes widen.

"Well, we're here to bring you up to my place to hang

67

out until the boys are done doing whatever it is they're doing," Abrianna tells me. "That way you can tell us about today. If you'd like, of course," she adds, giving me an out if I want one.

"That sounds nice, thanks." I don't really have any friends to have girl time with. I'm so isolated out on Staten Island, especially when I can only leave with my henchman as my driver and guard.

That's why I was so excited when I first met Tessa. I was excited to have another girl in the family. I mean sure, there are my cousins, but they all have their own lives. They get to have more freedoms than me since they're not a direct line to the boss.

Swinging my legs over the side of the bed, I wince when I stand, and they all take a step closer. "No, no, I'm fine." I wave them off. "I just haven't put any pressure on it yet. Dante carried me up here."

"Dante carried you up here?" Tessa asks, surprised.

"Yeah."

"Hmm…" she hums, and they all look at me with expectant faces.

"We'll talk upstairs," Abrianna says with a small smile, leading the way out.

I know what she's thinking. I know what they're all thinking. That Dante doesn't usually get close to people, touch people, or have hero moments of carrying someone to safety.

Grabbing my heels and purse from the chair beside the bed where Dante left them, I limp slowly after the three of them.

"Do you want to clean up and change?" Abrianna asks once we get inside of her and Leo's place. "I'm sure you want to get out of that dress."

"I really do."

"You two order food and pick out a movie," she says to Angela and Tessa, and loops her arm with mine. Abrianna walks me down the hall to the guest room's bathroom. "I'll leave some clean clothes on the bed for you. Take your time."

"Thanks, Abri. Truly, I really appreciate it."

"Of course." She smiles warmly before leaving, and I wonder, not for the first time, how my brother was able to get her, and keep her.

I find a ponytail on the sink's countertop and throw my hair up in a bun to wash my face first, and then take my blazer off and unzip my dress. Shimming out of it, I grab a washcloth from the shelf beside the vanity and sit on the edge of the bathtub to wet it. I add a little of the citrus scented bodywash that's on the small teak table beside the tub, careful as I clean my legs.

I try my best to wash this day off even though all I want to do is submerge in a hot bath with calming oils and a big glass of wine. When I'm done, I pat myself dry and then pad across the soft carpet of the bedroom to find a pair of light pink sweatpants and a white t-shirt laid out for me.

Stepping into the pants, I sigh. It feels good to put on something soft and comfortable.

I wish I knew what was going on downstairs with Dante and them. I've never been involved or present in anything involving my brothers or the family business like today. I've always been kept on the outskirts.

Were they aiming for me, my brothers, or all of us?

Do they know who did it?

Have they gone after him yet?

Pinching my eyes closed, I take a deep breath to try to remain calm. I have to find a way to get answers.

Folding my dress and blazer, I take them with me out to the living room and place them, and my shoes, down on the floor beside my purse.

"The food will be here soon," Abrianna informs me when I sit down. "Tell us what happened."

"Well, today was my lunch with Santino Antonucci. It was the first time I met the man my brothers want me to marry and I had an audience of testosterone-filled men who are always just one wrong look away from whipping their guns out."

"Sounds like a party," Tessa jokes.

"Oh, it was. Don't all good parties end with a hail of bullets? I was able to fake my way through lunch, smiling and having useless chit-chat with Santino, who was fine I guess, but I didn't feel anything for him. When he and his dad left, I started pacing towards the windows, which is when the first bullet struck the window of Giorgio's."

Angela flinches. "That's where I was brought when I had to meet with my brothers." Angela doesn't talk about her past much. All I know is that her family is the source of her pain, and her father is the one who had mine killed.

"After the first bullet pierced the glass…" I pause, shaking my head. "Everything went muted and time seemed to slow. But then another bullet came through the window and I felt my leg burn in a flash, and I fell to my hands and knees. I think. It's all kind of a blur. Bullets kept coming, and the window shattered as Dante ran to me. He covered me with his body to protect me."

I pause again, remembering how safe I felt under him. "And when the bullets stopped, he got me out of there and back here without any more problems. I don't know anything else. I wish I did, but I know no one is going to tell me anything. No one ever tells me anything. I may be a Carfano, but I'm not privy to any information. It's just my mom and I living in that big house…passing time."

"That sounds…" Tessa starts, then pauses.

"Boring?" I finish for her.

"Yes," she says ruefully, pity written all over her face.

"I've only had school, really. High school was horrible because my brothers scared everyone away from me. Girls included. Then I wasn't allowed to go to college in the traditional way, so I took as many online classes as possible, year-round, to keep me occupied. I was able to graduate early."

"Wait, when did you graduate?" Abrianna asks. "From where? With a degree in what?"

"I went to NYU for psychology, and I graduated this past summer," I tell her proudly, not having told anyone yet.

"That's really impressive," Angela says. "I'm going to be starting school again in the spring to finish my Art History degree."

"I loved my art history classes," I tell her, and she gives me a gracious smile.

"Wait," Abrianna chimes in. "How come I didn't know

this, Kat? Leo never mentioned you graduating."

"Oh, well, that's because I haven't told anyone yet."

"What?" all three of them exclaim at the same time.

"Why not?"

"I don't know. I mean, in the grand scheme of things, it didn't seem important. Things were happening with Alec and Tessa, and then Leo and Abri, and then Luca and Angela... There wasn't ever a time I wanted to try to celebrate *me*."

"I'm sorry, but no. You worked your ass off and graduated early. I'm getting us drinks to celebrate." Abri hops up and walks over to the bar cart where she grabs a bottle of wine and four glasses. She pours us each a hefty portion, but pauses before handing me mine. "You weren't given any hard pain killers, were you?" I shake my head and she clears her throat, raising her glass. "To Katarina. For surviving today *and* graduating college."

We all clink glasses as tears well in my eyes, and I'm unable to keep them from falling down my face. "Thank you."

"You're our sister, too," Tessa adds, and Angela grabs my hand, squeezing it. "I didn't have any family left before I met Alec, and now I have him and a whole family who has my back."

"Your brothers are going to be so proud of you," Abri tells me. "Telling them an accomplishment you're proud of should never be an inconvenience."

"I don't know why I kept it to myself. Maybe because it was something I did for myself, you know? It was for me. I know I'm not going to have a career from it or anything." I shrug. "I guess it kind of just felt like it wouldn't be a big deal to anyone other than me."

"I understand," Angela says. "I had nothing when I lived with my father. I had nothing but my books and school. They were the only two things I could control. Nothing else. They were the only things I had for *me*. Even if nothing comes of my degree either, it's still going to be an accomplishment. I hope to maybe, if I choose to, own or work at a gallery someday. But either way, it brings me a sense of self and independence to have control over my education."

The fact that she just opened up to us means so much to me.

"It seems we're a group of women hell-bent on doing our own thing." Tessa grins, just as a knock sounds at the front door, and she stands with Abri. "Which means we're your brothers' worst nightmares," she directs at me, making me huff out a short laugh.

"Yeah, my brothers have definitely found their matches. They need the challenge."

All four of us sit, eat, and watch a movie as I try not to think about today. But my leg starts to take on a heartbeat of its own after a while, which is when Leo walks in with Alec and Luca.

They each go to their woman to say hi and then turn to me. "How are you feeling?" Leo asks first.

"I'll be fine," I assure him. "But I'm tired…"

"I'll bring you to your apartment. I already sent mom to Miami and you'll stay here so I know you're safe."

"Alright," I agree, not finding any fault in his logic. I don't really want to go back to that house anyway.

Grabbing my things, I stand, and Leo comes right over

Rebecca Gannon

to take my bag and lend me his arm to lean on as I limp to the door.

"Wait a second," Abri says, jumping up and scurrying down the hall, returning a minute later with a duffel bag. "I packed you some things earlier to tie you over until you can get back to your house."

Leo takes it from her and slings it over his shoulder, giving her a grateful look.

"Thank you. For the clothes and tonight. I'll see you soon?"

"Definitely." Abri smiles, and I walk out with Leo.

"I'm really glad you're okay, Kat," he tells me as we step into the elevator.

"What did you find out? Do you know who did it?"

"Kat, please," Leo says, as if that's supposed to just be enough to shut me up.

"No, Leo, I don't want to be kept in the dark like always. I'm the one who got shot. I'm the one you're trying to marry off to some guy neither of us even knows. And you expect me to stay quiet through it all? I can't. I won't."

Leo assesses me. "All you have to worry about is healing. I'll take care of the rest."

"You're not hearing me, Leo."

"I am. But I don't want you to have to worry about it. You never should have been in danger today, and that's on me."

"It's not," I sigh, and give up the argument. "But you know what? I'm too tired to fight with you."

"Good," he says, and I internally roll my eyes.

We only go a few floors down, and when we step out of

74

the elevator, Leo walks me to one of two doors in the hallway. "Stefano added your prints and retinal scan to the system a long time ago, but this will be your code to punch into the elevator and this door. Don't get any ideas, though. The men down in the lobby know not to let you leave on your own."

"You think I want to run when I was just shot? I have nowhere to go, Leo." He lets me open the door myself and then steps into the apartment to make sure everything is as it should be.

"I sent someone out to grab you a few things for the fridge so you weren't completely empty, but you can make me a list of whatever you want and I'll have it brought to you."

"Thanks."

"If you need anything right away or if there's any trouble, Dante is right down the hall."

"He is?" I try to ask casually, but I'm not sure I pull it off.

"Yes. I trust him to protect you. He saved you today, Kat."

I clear the lump from my throat that has formed at the reminder of my almost demise today. "I know. I'm grateful."

Leo embraces me. "Get some rest."

"I will," I tell him, but after he leaves and I crawl into bed, all I can think about is the fact that Dante is right down the hall from me.

How am I supposed to rest knowing that?

CHAPTER 10
Katarina

Glass shatters and I scream.

My ears are ringing and my body is on fire, and all I feel is pain radiating from my chest. I press my hand to my sternum, feeling a warm wetness, and pull it away to see it covered in blood.

I fall to my knees.

Looking up, I see Dante's face stricken with shock as he runs towards me, falling to the floor in front of me. "Katarina. No. No, baby, no," he chants, taking me in his arms. He holds me close, his arms the only things keeping me together as I drift away.

Startled awake, I gasp for air and tear at the sheets that are tangled around me until I'm free.

My hands pat my torso, checking to make sure it was all

just a dream, and I clutch my chest, my pulse racing. My breath comes in quick pants. My brain isn't working, but I know where I want to go, and my feet carry me there. Right out of my apartment and down the hall to the only other door on this floor.

I lift my hand to knock on it, but stop, hearing piano music. I lean against the wall beside his door, sliding down until I hit the floor.

It's beautiful. Soothing.

It's bringing my heartbeat back into the right tempo as my breathing shallows out while I listen.

By the time the nightmare dissipates from my brain and I'm lulled back into a state of calm, the music stops, and I'm brought back to reality.

I wait a minute to see if it'll start again, but when it doesn't, I sigh, and manage to stand without putting too much weight on my injured leg. But in doing so, I accidentally bang my shoulder against the wall, which has Dante's door flying open in a matter of seconds.

And holy shit…

He's wearing a pair of black sweatpants and nothing else, and I can't do anything but stand here and take him in. My eyes roam over his torso and arms. He's covered in scars of all shapes, sizes, and stages of healing, and I want to reach out and touch them, but I don't.

His hair is a tousled mess, as if he was tossing and turning in bed and then ran his hands through it countless times. I want to do that. I want to see if it's as soft as it looks.

When my eyes finally meet his, they're scarily open to me. The two black holes are just begging to take me in.

"Are you okay, Katarina?"

"Yeah, I just… I had a bad dream and I came over here. But when I heard the music, I stopped to listen. I didn't mean to disturb you."

"You would never be disturbing me, Katarina. What was your dream about?"

"It was about today, but with a completely different outcome. Would you mind if I…?" I trail off, unsure if I should, or can, even ask him this. "I just really don't want to be alone in that apartment right now."

Taking a step back, Dante gives me the silent okay to enter. I hesitate, though. I know the moment I step in there, that's it for me. I'm sealing my fate to a man I have no business sealing my fate to. But before my brain can ever even weigh in on the debate, my feet are crossing the threshold. My heart and body win out for what they want.

Dante closes the door behind me and my eyes look around his place. The floors, furniture, countertops – everything is in shades of black, white, and grey. I expect nothing less from him. He seems like someone who's all about things being black and white, but then lives in the grey area.

"Do you want anything? Water? Coffee?"

"Do you have anything stronger than that?"

"I do."

Dante's apartment is spacious and open, and I watch him as he walks into the kitchen and takes two tumbler glasses from a cabinet. I carefully walk over to his couch, the dark hardwood floor cool under my feet, and the soft grey and white area rug warm, making me realize for the first time that I came over here barefoot.

Everything is neat and clean. Not that I ever pictured him as a messy person, but it's almost like he moved in and that was that. I don't see any personal touches. It's like a staged apartment made in his perfect color scheme.

I want to tuck my feet up under me, but the second I go to do so, my stitches pull and I suck in a sharp breath, letting my foot fall to the floor.

Dante puts the glasses down on the table and pours a little amber liquid in each. He hands me one and I take a sip immediately. "You're hurting."

"It's okay. I just forgot for a moment. It could be worse...like in my dream"

"What did you dream?"

"I dreamt that the bullet went through my chest instead of my leg. There was so much blood. I fell to my knees, and when I looked up, I saw you. You ran to me, but there was nothing you could do." I want to tell him that he held me, and that for a moment, I thought I would make it. But I don't. I can't.

I'm staring at the amber liquid swirling around in my glass when Dante's hands come into view and wrap around mine, stilling my movements. "Look at me."

My eyes travel up the length of his arms until I meet his, and like the liquor I was just swirling, they move, pulling me into them as if magnetized somehow, making me want to go deeper.

"Katarina," he starts, and a small sigh escapes me. I don't think I'll ever tire of hearing him say my name. He always says my full name, not just Kat, and it's beautiful. It's exotic coming from him because it's the only soft word that seems to ever leave his lips. "No one will hurt you. No one. As long as I'm around, you'll be safe."

"You can't promise me that."

"I can, and I am," he says matter-of-factly, as if it's such a simple statement. "If there's anyone who can promise you that, it's me. Everyone is afraid of me, babygirl. No one fucks with me and no one fucks with what's mine. And trust me when I say that I don't have anything else in this world that I consider mine. Just you. Do you hear me?"

"Yes…but…I'm not yours. I'm supposed to marry Santino…"

"The day you marry Santino, or anyone else, is a day that comes after I'm already rotting in the fucking ground. You're not marrying him. You were never going to marry him."

"I wasn't?"

"Things have been set in motion for a long time. I'm a patient man, Katarina, and I have been for years. It's been my own personal punishment to have to wait this long to have you. To know what your lips taste like. To know what sounds you make with my fingers inside of you. To know what it sounds like to have you beg for release. To know what your sweet virgin pussy tastes like. That's my heaven. The only one I know I'll get, and my reward for waiting so long. *And I've waited.* It's been fucking hell. And I'm still in hell because I know I still can't have you. Not all of you."

I think I just forgot how to breathe.

"I know you feel it, but I also know you're scared to feel it. Do you know the things I've done? What I do? And who I am for the family?"

"I…" I swallow.

"Your father nicknamed me The Executioner. I'm the enforcer. The hitter. I kill people. In fact, I killed someone just a few hours ago."

"What? Who?"

"Frank Antonucci. He's the one who set us up today."

I'm momentarily stunned. "So, that means Santino is the boss now? That means he still has the power to have me if Leo keeps the deal in place."

"He wants you, but he's not going to have you. And his grandfather is still the boss. Santino has no power."

"Doesn't Leo need the deal to go through?"

"The deal can still go through," he says, and my heart drops. "Just not with you," he finishes.

"What do you mean?"

"I'll take care of it. I'll take care of you." His fingers graze up my forearm and back to my wrist. He repeats the path, lulling me into a state of calm by the simplest of touches. It's gentler than I ever imagined he could be and probably ever has been. Now combine his eyes with his hypnotic touch, and I'm falling into a state of mind where nothing around me feels real besides us.

"You came here after your dream. Why?"

"Because I wanted you to make me feel better."

"Do you still want me to?"

"Yes," I sigh.

He takes the drink out of my hand and places it on the glass table, which he pushes out of the way so he can kneel at my feet. The sight of him getting down to my eye level feels like taming the beast just the slightest. But taming Dante is the last thing that I want to do. I want to feel all of him unleashed on me.

"I've been waiting years to taste you firsthand, Katarina. *Years.* I've licked my fingers clean, but I want to drink straight from the source."

"So, if I asked you years ago to touch me, to kiss me, to taste me, you would have?"

"No."

"Why not?"

"You never would have asked me years ago. You needed the threat of losing everything to finally ask for what you want."

It hurts to hear him say it, but I know he's right. I never would have asked him years ago, and I still haven't. Not really. I was looking at a future with a man I didn't want, so I played with and baited Dante into giving me exactly what I wanted.

And it worked.

But I can see in his eyes now that he wants me to ask him. He wants me to finally be who've I've wanted to be and who he knew I could be. His.

"Touch me, Dante." His eyes flare with dark heat. "Put your hands on me. Put your mouth on me. Everywhere."

"Is that you asking?"

"Did you hear a question?"

"No."

"Then I'm not asking. I'm telling you what I want."

The corner of his mouth lifts in a small smirk that has my heart lurching in my chest.

"Whatever you want, babygirl, I'll give you."

His hands slide up my thighs to grip the waistband of my sweatpants, and I lift my hips as he slowly pulls them down. He's careful to avoid the bandages on my left calf, but then glides his finger around the perimeter of the tape and gauze, almost in a trance of his own.

Blinking out of it, Dante finishes taking my pants off and then slides his hands up the backs of my calves, gripping me behind my knees to spread my legs apart.

His eyes are between my thighs when he takes a deep breath. "So fucking perfect," he murmurs.

Leaning in, he skims his nose along my inner thigh, his shoulders holding me open. He blows cool air against my core and I shiver, biting my lip to hold back my moan.

"Let me hear you, Katarina. This isn't the car. You can be as loud as you want. The louder the better. Got it?"

I nod, and he rewards me with his hot tongue slashing up my slit. I scream, not prepared for the onslaught.

"That's more like it."

And as if it's his goal to make me scream even louder, he doesn't let up on me. His tongue swirls around my clit, making my legs quiver every time he flicks it with the tip of his tongue.

Moaning, I reach out to grip the edges of the cushion on either side of me, needing to anchor myself. I'd grip his hair or shoulders, but I don't want him to lose focus. I don't want him to stop.

His tongue glides down and circles my entrance, but he doesn't go any further, and I grunt out my frustration.

"You'll take what I give you," he growls out, his teeth scraping down both sides of my pussy lips. My clit throbs, begging for him to give me more, but he still just teases me.

I'm blind and deaf to everything but the pleasure rippling through me, radiating out from where his mouth touches me.

He spreads me wider, giving him greater access to me, and I've never felt so open, so exposed, or so vulnerable.

He keeps teasing me. Nibbling, scraping, and sucking his way up and down my pussy, swirling his tongue around my clit, but never breaching my entrance.

It's too much, and yet not enough.

"Dante, please," I moan, begging him to let me come.

I grow wetter and wetter, to where I feel myself leaking down between my ass cheeks like a river. I didn't even know it was possible to be this wet and this turned on.

He presses my knees to my chest, lifting my hips off the couch to lick the come that's escaped him, scooping it up. "All of this is mine, babygirl. I'm not wasting a single fucking drop," he says roughly, biting my ass cheek.

"Dante, please," I beg again.

"Tell me what you want. I want to hear you say it."

"I want you inside me. Your tongue. Your fingers. Either. Both. Please. Now."

I'm looking down at him between my thighs and I see that little spark in his eyes return right before he shoves his tongue inside of me, plugging me with it while he presses down on my clit with his thumb.

He sucks hard, sucking the life out of me. Stars dot my vision and my head thrashes against the back of the couch. "Oh my God, oh my God," I chant, and Dante releases me.

"God's not with you, babygirl. I am."

"Dante," I moan.

"That's fucking right. You say *my* name when I'm eating the pussy that's mine. Not God's. *Mine.*"

"Yours," I sigh, and he grazes his teeth over my clit, making me scream.

"Your screams are mine, too. Your pussy is mine. Your body is mine. *You're mine.* Always have been."

"Yes."

"Say it," he demands.

"I'm yours."

"That's fucking right."

Shoving his fingers inside of me, he sucks on my tight bundle of nerves, and I can't take anymore. I scream his name and squeeze his shoulders with my thighs, wrapping my legs around him. My body is completely at his mercy and under his control, and I have no idea what's happening to me. It's as if I'm floating and flying, but drowning at the same time.

When I finally resurface, it's Dante's beard scraping against my inner thighs and his dark eyes piercing mine that catch me. I have to blink to get mine in focus.

"Dante…" I whisper, shaking my head, at a loss for words.

"I'll worship you every chance you give me."

Pushing my legs apart, he stands over me and kisses me hard, letting me taste myself on his lips and tongue. It's dirty and hot, and I know there's so much that he can show and teach me, and I want it all.

"Your virgin pussy tastes so sweet, babygirl. The only pussy I've ever needed and will ever need. It's going to be *my* cock that stretches you open for the first time, and there will be no mistaking that I've claimed you." My breath hitches in my throat as his nose slides across my jaw and his teeth pull on my ear lobe. "How does that sound, Katarina? Being fully mine?"

His breath is warm against my ear and I sigh, his scent enveloping me. I'm dizzy from being so close to him. I'm dizzy from having his mouth on me. And I'm dizzy from his words. I've always wanted to be his.

"I already am," I manage to whisper, and he groans, scraping his teeth down the column of my neck. He pulls back to look at me, cupping my throat possessively.

"You're not fully mine, but you will be. You'll know when you are."

"When?" I practically pant, my core throbbing, wanting exactly what he's saying, exactly what he's promising. He rubs his thumb up and down the side of my throat. "You said I've always been yours. Why not make it now?"

"Because I have to talk to Leo. He already has a reason to kill me. I'm not giving him a second one."

"What?"

"I've done things, Katarina."

"What are you talking about? What have you done?"

His jaw clenches and his lips press together, so I reach up and cup his cheek and he instantly relaxes. I run my finger down his scar and he closes his eyes briefly. When they open again, he lets me see inside. He lets me see how deep he goes, which makes me know that whatever he's done is bad.

"I did what was needed, and I always will. I would do anything for you, Katarina."

"What did you do?" I ask again, almost afraid to know, but needing to all the same.

"I saw when your looks changed towards me," he says instead of answering my question. "You were terrified of me at first. Then, one day you were a little less terrified. And it kept lessening until I saw in your eyes exactly how I felt."

"What did you see?"

His thumb continues to caress my throat. "Need." He presses into me, his eyes flaring.

We stay locked together for a moment longer before Dante pulls away and kneels back down at my feet. He slides my sweatpants back up, careful when lifting them over my wrapped calf.

"Do I have to go back?"

"You're safe here. Our security rivals the government's. You know that, right?"

"I know," I whisper, when what I really want to tell him is that I don't want to leave him. I don't want to be alone in that apartment.

I'm about to give in and resign myself to a night by myself when he offers, "I have a guest room you can sleep in."

"Guest room?"

"Yes, Katarina. You can't sleep in my bed. I only possess so much restraint. It's the guest room or you go back to your apartment."

"Alright. I'll stay in your guest room." Dante helps me up from the couch, and as we walk down the hall, we pass a second, smaller living room area that has a grand piano in it. "Was that you playing earlier?" I thought it was just music he was playing, not actually him.

"Yes."

"I didn't know you played. You never played at the house."

"No, I didn't. I started again when I moved in here."

"These apartments come with pianos? The one I'm in doesn't have one, and neither do my brothers'."

"No. Arrangements were made."

"Leo knows you play?"

"He didn't ask. People tend to not ask questions about me."

"Can I?"

"You're the only one. But be careful what you ask. Because I'm never going to lie to you and you may not like the answers you get."

"Will you play for me some time?"

Stopping just outside of a door, he turns to me and lifts my chin with two fingers. "Get some rest."

"I'll try."

Dante steps away and shoves his hands into the pockets of his sweatpants, and my eyes dart down to get another eyeful of him before slipping inside the room and closing the door behind me.

I head straight for the bed and crawl up onto it. It's comfortable, but too big and too empty. I've slept alone my entire life, but this is different. I try my left side, my right side, my back, and my stomach, but all I can think about is Dante and how he wants to make me his.

When I can't take it anymore, I throw the covers off and walk to the door, then walk back to the bed, unsure of what I should do.

Taking a deep breath, I walk back to the door and this time make it out into the hall. In front of the door next to mine, I raise my hand to knock, but then lower it.

If I do this...

I raise my hand again and knock lightly. It takes a few seconds, but the door opens and Dante is standing there...completely naked...with his dick in his hand.

CHAPTER 11
Dante

Katarina's going to be the death of me, testing my restraint the way she is. I shouldn't have agreed to let her stay in the room next door.

She closes the door and I curl my hands into fists, stalking down the hall to my room. Shedding my clothes, I turn the shower on and step under the spray of water, making it as cold as possible. The freezing temperature does nothing to tamp down how hard my fucking dick is. It never does.

I've taken cold showers because of Katarina for at least six fucking years now, and I've come to relish in them. They keep me numb to everything while I beat my cock into oblivion just to take the edge off.

That's all I've ever been able to do – take the edge off.

Nothing short of being inside of Katarina will ever satisfy me, and I know once I get inside of her, I won't be able to leave until both of us pass the fuck out. I have years of going without to catch up on.

Fisting myself, I press my other hand to the tiles and close my eyes, seeing my girl spread open for me on my couch behind my lids.

Fuck, she's beautiful.

Her pussy leaked for me and I lapped that shit up. I can't wait to see how much she'll drip for me next time before I let her come.

She tastes so fucking good. A sweet and salty dessert.

God may have given up on me a long time ago, and I Him, but He made her, and she's made for me.

I lick my lips and I can still taste her. Squeezing the base of my cock, I picture her squeezing me the way she did my fingers and tongue inside of her, and I blow my fucking load all over the shower wall.

I quickly scrub myself clean and then step out of the shower, toweling off. I don't bother putting anything on, because with Katarina right next door, I know my cock won't get any rest tonight.

Whenever I can't sleep, I play the piano, but I don't want to wake her up, so I revert to lying on my bed in the dark with my eyes closed, drumming my fingers on my legs to a tune I know well.

I can hear the music perfectly in my head as if I was really playing, and my cock grows stiffer and stiffer as the minutes pass, until I'm so fucking hard, I have to take myself in my hand again.

Grunting, I start out slow, my mind filled with Katarina's face while she orgasmed, and the feel of her legs squeezing my shoulders.

I'm lost in my visions of everything I want to do to her when a light knock on the door pulls me back to the here and now.

Rolling off the bed, I take long strides to the door and fling it open, still gripping my dick.

"Is something wrong?" I ask immediately, her eyes wide as she takes me in. They roam over my arms and chest before landing on my hand wrapped around myself.

"I...I didn't mean to interrupt..." she stammers, swallowing hard.

"This is what you do to me," I grunt, and her eyes flit up to mine. "You want to watch what you do to me?"

Her eyes go right back down to my hand. "I..."

"You're playing with fire, babygirl." I pump my length once, twice...

"I couldn't sleep. I was thinking about..." she starts, then stops, licking her lips.

"About what?"

"You." She pauses again, taking a small step towards me. "I..."

"You can't come in here," I growl roughly, and she jumps back. "If you come in here, I won't be gentle or nice with you, and I don't want to be. But it's what you need while you're hurt." She swallows hard, her eyes still on my dick. "You're not ready to come in here, Katarina. Not yet."

"Will you...keep going?" she asks boldly, her eyes

darting up to mine and then back down to my hand.

Fuck me.

If my girl wants to watch me fuck myself, then I'm going to fuck myself, this time not having to imagine her face while I do it.

Gripping the top of the door frame, I keep my eyes on her face, not wanting to miss a single look or emotion that passes across it.

She looks fascinated, eager, and curious, and even though I wish to holy hell that I could be fucking her right now, I would never complain. Especially since she's hurt. And having her watch me fuck my hand, knowing she knows it's all for her, makes my dick even harder.

I stroke myself slowly at first, but when she licks her lips, scraping the bottom one with her teeth, I fist my cock and rock my hips into my hand. Katarina's breath hitches and she stumbles back until she hits the wall across from me.

My hand's grip on the door frame is so tight, I'm surprised I haven't split the goddamn wood. My hips thrust into my hand, mimicking fucking the beautiful woman in front of me. And by the sound of her rapid breathing, I know she's envisioning the same thing.

I grunt and her eyes flash up to mine, showing me everything. She's so fucking turned on.

Come leaks out the tip of my cock and I twist my fist as I thrust. Katarina's glazed-over eyes run down the length of me, starting at my hand gripping the door frame. My girl likes what she sees, and I love knowing that. Because for the years I've had to go without her, I've imagined every scenario and outcome between us. Both her wanting me just as much as I want her, and her not wanting anything to do with me. That thought won out more times than I'd like to admit, and usually did when I hadn't seen her in a while.

I thrust my hips faster and fire licks down my spine.

Katarina's thighs rub together. I know she's soaking wet, which has the fire flaming across my skin and my cock stiffening until I fucking blow, my come shooting out of me and landing on the floor between us. Katarina gasps and stares down at it, her chest rising and falling in quick breaths.

Stepping over my release, I hold my hand up to her lips where some of my come dripped onto. "Lick me clean. Taste what you do to me."

Katarina reaches up and takes my wrist, licking my fingers and palm clean. "What do I taste like, Katarina?"

"I don't know," she whispers. "Salty. It's good."

"Next time, I'm going to shoot my come down your throat. It seems wasted on the floor now, doesn't it?"

She gives me a small nod.

Brushing the backs of my fingers down her cheek, her eyes flutter closed and I kiss her. "Go back to your room and try to sleep," I tell her, and step back into my room.

CHAPTER 12

Dante

I woke up to find Katarina gone. The bed was made and nothing was out of place, making it seem as if she was never here. If it weren't for the vivid memories of last night ingrained in my mind, I might believe it was all a dream. But there's no way I imagined eating her pussy on my couch and jacking off while she watched.

Checking my phone, I see Leo messaged me over an hour ago to meet him down in the conference room. Shit. After she watched me last night, I was able to finally pass the fuck out, and I slept longer than I have in a long fucking time. Probably because I came so damn hard, I had no choice.

Showering, I dress in what I always do — a black button-down shirt and black trousers. Black doesn't show blood.

I don't like that she left without saying anything, but I don't know what I would do if she was here. I want nothing short of everything with her, and pretending like I don't is impossible. I want to walk into my kitchen after a night of fucking to find her wearing one of my shirts and drinking coffee. One of us will make breakfast and then we'll fuck again on the counter because the way her mouth moves as she chews is too fucking sexy to resist.

But I have to talk to Leo. When, how, and what I'll say? I don't know. But I owe him that. I owe the family that respect.

I almost knock on Katarina's apartment door on my way, but I know if I see her before meeting Leo, I won't make it down there. But when I do get down to the conference room, I find Katarina seated at one end of the table, away from her brothers and cousins.

"What's going on?"

"Where have you been?" Leo asks. "I texted you over an hour ago and you never answered."

"I'm here now. Did you find out something new?" There are plenty of empty seats around the table, yet I take the one beside Katarina, gaining curious looks from everyone.

Looking directly at Leo, I challenge him to say something about it, but he doesn't. His eyes slide from me to Katarina, and then back to me. They don't change. His face is devoid of any and all emotion, shielding his thoughts.

I'm not leaving Katarina to sit across from her family, believing it's her against them. I know she's more than capable of handling herself with them because she's a Carfano herself, which means the ruthless genes are woven into her DNA just as tightly as any of them. But that doesn't mean I'm going to leave her to believe she's alone in her fight. I fought for her when she didn't know I was, and now I'm going to fight right alongside her.

Stefano rubs his left eye and takes a gulp of coffee from the mug beside him. "I stayed up all night, searching every corner of the web for any information and trail of Hovan I could find. He's been busy trying to rebuild what we destroyed. Several men connected to the family back in Armenia arrived in New York last month, all listing the same address on their arrival cards."

"Then why don't we go there now?" Nico questions.

"Because that's not all. Hovan put out a hit on all of us, and the man he hired is linked to a bunch of hits across Europe, Russia, and North Africa. He's known as The Ghost."

"I've heard of him," I tell them.

"How?" I look at Nico with a blank stare and he shakes his head. "Of course. Why do I bother asking?"

"He's ex-Armenian military and the best sniper to come out of there in the last two decades. He's never been linked to anything in America, though."

"So we're literally chasing a ghost?" Luca asks. "How do we find him?"

"We hire him ourselves," Alec suggests. "Draw him out."

"He'll see through that," I tell them. "Two hits in the same city within days of each other when he's never been here before? And it's a hit on the man who hired him for the first job? No, he'll just collect the money and either run or kill us all. Well, try to," I correct.

"Then what do you suggest?"

"We find Hovan first," Leo says before I can. "He has to have a way to contact or find The Ghost, and then we take care of him and send his family back home. Kat, you'll stay here until this is all done with."

"And then?" she asks.

"And then you'll marry Santino as planned," Leo tells her, as if that was ever in question.

My fists clench under the table as she forcefully says, "No."

"Excuse me?" Leo's eyebrows raise, surprised.

"You heard me. I'm not marrying him. I could barely stand a lunch with him, and I refuse to extend that to my whole life. I can't even fathom the idea of him touching me."

I swallow the growl that threatens to rumble from my chest. No one's fucking touching her.

"Kat," Leo warns, and from the corner of my eye, I see her visibly flinch.

"No," she says fiercely. "Don't. You don't need me to make some deal go through. And if you do, then maybe you're not that good at leading this family." This time it's Leo's turn to flinch. "You can either figure out another way or let the deal fall through. Is the money more important than me? You tell me right now if it is and I'll walk right out of here and you'll never see me again."

Grinding my jaw, I turn my head to look at her and her eyes meet mine, the fiery halo in them burning bright. She's so goddamn beautiful. I knew she had fight in her. She's been kept quiet her entire life, but I always knew she was far from meek, weak, or pliant to whatever her family had in store for her.

Even the most beautiful and sweet-natured of creatures fights back when they're cornered and faced with only one way out.

"I deserve to have what all of you have. A choice. A choice in who I marry. A choice in who I love."

Her words make my fucking chest twist.

Love.

That word hadn't meant much to me until I let myself *feel* for Katarina. Now it's synonymous with utter obsession, protection, and the need to be as close to her as possible.

She's the reason I still hear music in my head.

She's the reason my heart keeps on beating when it should have stopped a long time ago.

"We need to keep the peace, Kat. We can't go around breaking deals that have been in place for years."

"Then have someone else marry him. I'm not the only woman in this family. Why haven't you offered your sister, Nico? Maybe Mia will like him. Or Gia, Aria, or Elena. It doesn't have to be me."

Leo rubs his jaw, thinking her words over while Nico remains quiet on the mention of his sister taking Katarina's place as the sacrificial lamb.

"I see you've never bothered to think of that." Standing, Katarina pushes one side of her hair over her shoulder. "I'll leave you to do just that. Because if the only reason you're still having me do this is because our father made a promise to them over five years ago, then that's a bullshit reason and you know it."

Walking out of the room, I stare after her, so fucking proud.

CHAPTER 13
Katarina

Walking out of the conference room, I huff out a breath in frustration and frantically push the elevator button until it opens — a little déjà vu from not so long ago.

I'm tempted to take it down to the garage and just walk the hell out of here, but I can't. I can't leave when things are only just getting started with Dante.

At my apartment door, I press in the code, but hesitate with my hand on the handle, looking down the hall at Dante's door. I don't know when he's coming back, but I really don't want to sit alone in my apartment just *waiting*. For something. Anything.

Besides, I have a feeling Dante isn't going to keep me

waiting long.

Sliding down the wall beside his door, I close my eyes, taking a deep breath. I hate feeling so out of sorts and out of control. I'm not used to this anger and resentment taking root in my core and staying there. It's as if a switch flipped in me and I'm suddenly seeing my life for what it's been and what I've settled for. My father may have suppressed my voice, but he's not here anymore, and I'm not letting Leo think he can treat me the same way any longer.

It's maybe ten or fifteen minutes later that I hear the ding of the elevator. "Katarina?" Dante asks, his long legs striding towards me. "Why are you out here?"

"I didn't want to sit in my apartment. I just…" Running my hands through my hair, I grip it at my scalp. "I feel like I have no control over anything that's happening in my life right now. It was never something I had complete control over, but I at least had *some*. Now, in the past two days, I've had to face the man Leo wants me to marry, I've been shot at, I all but threw myself at you and you still said no, and—"

"Stop," he says, cutting me off. Squatting down so he's at my eye level, Dante pinches my chin between his thumb and forefinger. "First off, don't even for a second think I wanted to say no to you. I've wanted to be with you for longer than you possibly know. And I *will* have you," he says firmly. "You wanting me as desperately as I do you is a fucking dream, Katarina. *A fucking dream.*" He has me held captive under his intense gaze. "Now, I know exactly what you need. Stand up."

Holding his hand out for me, I place mine in his and he helps me stand, the look in his eyes making my stomach knot.

"Where are we going?" I ask him as we walk back to the elevator.

"You'll see." I give him a questioning look when he has us going to the basement, and he repeats, "You'll see."

We ride down the entirety of the building, and the men in the gym area immediately turn to stare at me when I walk in. I'm pretty sure they've never seen a girl down here, and certainly never me — the boss's sister.

"Dante, I'm not dressed to work out, and to be honest, I really don't want to."

"You're not here to work out."

I look around as I follow him, gaining head nods of respect from those I make eye contact with. I'm not used to being viewed as a woman who holds power, but I guess I am. I just haven't been allowed to use or feel it.

Dante leads me down another hall, past a shooting range, and then over to a door that he punches in a code to access that's different from the one I've seen him use in the elevator. He holds the door open for me and my eyes widen, taking in all the guns and weapons, my leg automatically throbbing just being near them.

"Why are we here?"

"I'm helping you take your power back." He steps up close behind me, his next words spoken low in my ear. "And it's a great tension reliever."

"We could just have a repeat of last night to relieve some tension," I whisper, my body buzzing with the need to feel his hands and mouth all over me again.

"Not yet," he says, his breath blowing across my ear,

sending a shiver through me.

Dante walks up to the wall and picks out a smaller handgun and grabs a box of bullets before raising his chin to follow him back out to the range.

I watch him get the gun ready, sliding the pieces apart and back together again, inspecting it. You'd think after yesterday, I'd have a fear of guns, but I've grown up knowing every man that came through the house and worked for my father had one hidden beneath his suit jacket.

I've also been going down to the range my father had in the basement of the back house on our property for a few years now. It was where my brothers, cousins, Dante, and all of my father's soldiers would go to train and prove themselves to him. My father demanded respect and obedience from everyone under him, and I know it all started in that building.

It took me two years after his death to find the courage to go inside of it. A few men went in the week after he died, but then never again. They had to have been cleaners of some kind, because the place was clean. Too clean. For what I think must have happened in there, there should have been *some* kind of evidence left behind. But every surface was spotless, save for a fine layer of dust.

As I kept exploring, I found it eerie. There were rooms with nothing more than a chair and restraints. There were rooms similar to the gym setup here in this building for fighting I presume, and when I made it to the basement, I found an arsenal of weapons along with a shooting range for practice. The weapons were hidden in a false paneling I discovered, and after that, I pretty much taught myself.

No one knew where I was or what I was doing because the cameras on the estate didn't cover the building. My father was big on privacy and didn't like the idea of anyone having the ability to spy on him. I'm assuming the house was kept fully stocked as a place to retreat to in case anything ever went down and we'd need to defend ourselves behind those walls.

I'll eventually have to tell Leo that I've used quite a bit of ammo over the past three years, testing out different guns. But that's for another day. I've become more than adept with a handgun, and I'm pretty proud of that. Which is why I know I'm about to surprise Dante.

"Grab a pair of new ear plugs from the table over there," he instructs, and then grips the barrel of the gun and holds the handle out for me to take. I inspect it, testing the weight in my hand. "Turn and face the target." I do as he says, playing along like I don't know what I'm doing, and he steps up behind me. Pulling one ear plug out that I just put in, he calmly tells me, "Spread your legs so you have a solid base, raise your arms, find the target, take a breath, and"—he brings his lips close to my ear—"be prepared to feel the shot's vibrations run through you."

He places the plug back in my ear and my neck breaks out in a flush of goosebumps from just the brush of his fingertips.

Taking a deep breath, I relax my shoulders and step my feet apart. I can feel him behind me, causing a surge of nerves to bubble up from never having shot a gun in front of anyone before. I want to impress him. I want to show him that I can be a part of this area of his life. I'm not some helpless woman.

I push the nerves away and wait for the familiar rush of adrenaline to course through me that always does when I realize the power in my hands. My body winds up in anticipation, and on my next exhale, I pull the trigger.

The familiar aftershocks rush through me and my pulse thrums with excitement.

Taking another breath, I pull the trigger again, and then again and again until I'm out of bullets, feeling myself regaining some of the control I felt I've lost. It's always within me, though. I just have to summon it.

I put the gun on the ledge in front of me and Dante steps up behind me, pulling my ear plugs out. "You've been keeping secrets, Katarina," he rasps, pressing his hips into my back so I can feel how hard he is.

Did me shooting a gun turn him on?

"I'm a woman. I have to have a few secrets for you to discover."

"Who taught you how to shoot?"

"I did."

Gripping my hips, Dante pulls me back and spins me around to press me against the wall behind us. He looks both confused and impressed. "Explain. Because that was the sexiest fucking thing you could've done in that moment, babygirl. You hit the target dead center every time."

Smiling, I lick my dry lips and watch his eyes follow the motion. "I went into the back house three years ago to see what was in there and found the hidden panel with the weapons beside the range. I knew no one would know or find me, and really, what would someone say? I'm not allowed to play with the family guns?"

"*Fuck*," he groans, pressing his forehead to mine. "I thought I knew everything about you, but here you are, surprising me."

"Why would you think you know everything about me?"

"Because I've been watching you," he tells me, as if it's such a normal thing to reveal. "I've spent every free moment I've had going on six years now, watching you through the security cameras on the compound. I had a few hidden ones along the wall turned towards the property so I could make sure you were safe."

Instead of being creeped out, a warmth spreads through my chest. I always felt like I was being watched when I would roam around outside, and now I know why.

"But you never saw me go into the back house?"

"None of the cameras were pointed there."

"Thank you," I whisper, tilting my head up so my lips brush against his. "You were protecting me when I didn't even know it. When I thought no one cared about me."

His grip on my waist tightens. "You should never have felt that way."

"I don't anymore," I tell him honestly, and he slams his mouth down on mine in a kiss that literally makes my heart stop beating for a moment. I can feel him pouring things he wants to say to me into it. That *he* cares. That he *has* cared.

I didn't know it, but I do now.

CHAPTER 14
Katarina

"What else can you show me down here to help me feel more in control?" I ask Dante when I catch my breath. "Because right now, my control is hanging by a thread."

Brushing his stubbled cheek against mine, he swirls his tongue around my ear and I sigh. "I'll start with my favorite," he says roughly.

"Which is?"

"I'll show you."

I follow him out of the range and back down the hall to another door off the main gym area. Dante closes and locks the door behind us and I turn to look at the door and then him. "What are you doing?"

"Making sure no one interrupts."

"Why? What do you plan on teaching me?"

"How to have control." He steps up to me, dragging his finger down my jaw. "And then how to let go of it. Do you want me to teach you?" I nod my head yes, wanting to learn anything he's willing to teach me. "Good girl," he praises, and my heart lurches at those two simple words. I want to be good for him, but I also want to be so damn bad with him.

Stepping around me, Dante walks off to a cabinet in the corner of the room where he pulls out a wrapped bundle of some kind and then returns to me. Placing it on a small metal table, he rolls it out, revealing a set of knives, each in their own slot.

I finally look around the room we're in and see a line of wooden targets on one wall, all in different shapes and sizes. Including ones shaped like people.

"Your specialty is knife throwing?"

"My specialty is everything, babygirl. But knives are my favorite. They're quieter than guns. And more personal." The hairs on my arms stand on end when he says this, giving me a glimpse into the man he is for my family.

He prefers knives to guns. The man who doesn't like to get close to anyone and always keeps his distance, prefers a more personal way of killing and torturing.

Except he gets close to me. And when he does, all I feel from him is his desire to bring me pleasure, not pain. He wants to take the pain out of my life, not give me more.

"I'm going to show you first, and then you're going to try."

"Okay," I say softly, wanting to see him in his element. I

step out of his way and notice tape marked off at different distances on the floor. Dante steps on the farthest piece. It's maybe fifty or sixty feet away from the target, perhaps even more.

He picks up one of the knives — a double-edged blade that's so smooth and shiny, it catches the light from the fluorescents overhead. The handle is an intricate black twisted metal that's rounded off at the end. It's beautiful.

Dante rolls his shoulders back and raises his arm, bringing his forearm and hand back before snapping it forward. It all happens too quickly, and the sound of the knife hitting the target makes me flinch.

He turns to look at me, and keeping his eyes on mine, he throws the next one. I turn to look where it landed, and it's dead center, right beside the previous one.

"How did you...?" I trail off, amazed by his abilities. He doesn't answer me, instead throws one after another, all the while keeping his gaze locked with mine.

With each impact of a knife hitting the target, I feel it like a hit to my core, making me throb.

"Now it's your turn," he says, walking up to the target and pulling the six knives free.

"Can I try it closer?" I ask, and Dante moves the table to half the distance he threw from and lays the knives back out. "These are beautiful. I don't want to ruin them by missing the target."

"I had them custom made. Believe me, they can take a drop to the floor."

"Alright."

Dante stands close behind me as I pick one of them up.

He covers my hand gripping the handle with his own and runs it up my arm. "Feel the weight of it in your hand just like the gun. Feel it as an extension of your own hand. Feel the purpose of it — to have the blade lodge into your target. It's all in the wrist. You'll eventually know how much power to put behind your throw based on distance, but this is your first time," he murmurs in my ear. "Just do what feels right."

I swallow hard, my concentration waning with how close he is. Dante steps away and I feel his loss, but then come to feel his residual energy and power left behind in the knife and in my hand, and I want to use it.

I bring my hand up around my ear and take a breath, letting my heart rate slow. I close one eye and then the other, seeing my target. When I feel as confident as I'll get, I bring my arm down and flick my wrist. But sadly, to no avail, the handle hits the target and the knife clammers to the cement floor.

I huff out a breath and pick up another knife. Dante doesn't say anything, he just stands by me and lets me figure it out for myself.

Rolling my shoulders back, I stretch my neck out and bring my arm back a little farther this time, giving me more leverage. This time when I throw it, it catches the bottom of the target, but still falls to the floor.

Grunting, I grab the next one and fling it without thought, and it stabs the very top of the target.

"Oh my God, I did it!" I say excitedly, turning to Dante. His lips turn up slightly and he gives me a nod of praise that has my chest warming.

"Good job. Try again."

With more confidence, I pick up another knife and throw it without thought again, but I miss. Again. Pursing my lips, I throw the last two in quick succession, not really caring, and they both stick. Neither hits the bullseye by any means, but they still make it onto the target.

"I guess I only do well when I'm pissed off," I huff out on a small laugh.

"You tried to control your body and you missed. When you gave control over to the knife, you hit the target."

"Are you trying to make a metaphor here?"

He lifts one shoulder in a shrug. "You can take it however you'd like. You're always fully in control, Katarina. But that control needs to be transferred to the knife and the task at hand to find your accuracy. Don't let your brain get too involved. It can be too powerful."

"So, don't think, just feel?"

"Yes. To an extent."

"In that case…" Walking up to him, I grip his shirt in my fist and lift up on my toes, kissing him until I lose my breath. "Thanks for the advice."

His hand grips my waist, keeping me close. "Go stand by the first body target," he rasps, releasing me.

"What?" I breathe, not thinking I heard him correctly.

"The first body target. Go. Now."

"You want me to stand in front of it? Why?"

"Stop asking questions and do as I say."

"Dante…"

Taking my elbow, he brings me in close and cups my face. "Do you trust me?"

I search his eyes. "Why would you ask that?"

"Because it's important. Do you trust me?"

"Yes, of course I do," I tell him, and he brushes his fingers down my cheek.

"I would never hurt you, Katarina. I want to show you something. I want to do something I've thought about for years."

"Okay," I whisper, and line myself up in front of the target while he collects his knives and moves the table over to line up with this target. He twists one around in his hand and I begin to tremble, not exactly sure if I want to do this. Dante sees my fear and he stalks towards me with the knife still in his hand.

"Why are you afraid, babygirl?"

"I'm not," I lie, and he levels me with a look.

"You said you trust me. This will only work if you truly do."

"I do," I say softly, but my voice waivers. "I just don't like the idea of being your target."

"You're not my target, Katarina. You're my beautiful painting in need of a frame." Raising the knife in his hand, he shows me the blade. "It's only dangerous if I want it to be. There's a fine line between pleasure and pain, but there's also a fine line between being put in a dangerous situation and feeling fear, or being turned on. I've never tested the second one. I want to with you. Will you let me?"

Dante places the cold flat side of the blade to my cheek and I don't flinch. The chill of the metal runs through me, pooling in my core.

"I see the reaction in your eyes, babygirl. Your pussy is getting wet, isn't it?" he asks, his voice low and deep.

"Yes," I sigh, and he turns the blade, skirting the edge over my cheek and down my neck. His featherlight touch reminds me of just how sharp the blade is, and how just a little pressure into my skin, or if I flinch or turn my head, the blade would cut right into me.

He's right. The possible danger should have me scared, and with anyone else I would be, but not with Dante. My pulse is racing and I'm acutely aware of the man doing it to me. I'm so turned on. My pussy is throbbing and my panties are soaked, wanting him to run the blade over my entire body.

"I'm glad you're wearing a dress. It makes what I'm about to do much easier."

Dante reaches around me, pulling the zipper of my dress down. "Arms out," he instructs as he pulls my dress down to my hips. Reaching back around me, he unclasps my bra and drops it to the floor.

My nipples pebble under his scrutiny, aching for his attention. "Your tits are perfect." Lowering his head, he captures one with his mouth and swirls his tongue around the tight bud until it's painfully hard, then does the same with the other.

Releasing me with a wet pop, he blows air across both of my nipples, making them stiffen further. Moaning, Dante scrapes the blade over my right nipple and then presses the cold flat side to it. I cry out, the sensation like a bolt of lightning through me with the mix of temperatures. My skin flushes as my blood rushes to the surface, making the metal feel like ice against me.

He repeats the process with my left nipple, and I lose my

mind. "Dante," I moan, my back arching off the target.

"In the right hands, anything can be a weapon, and anything can be foreplay. You're so fucking beautiful," he muses, his eyes roaming all over me. "So fucking beautiful. The way you react to me. The way your skin flushes when you're turned on. The way your nipples harden into the most perfect little buds for me that I could suck on all day. Then there's the heaven between your legs that's so sweet for me. Only me."

Dante circles my nipples with the round end of the handle, then slides it down the center of my stomach and up under the skirt of my dress. He slides it up and down my inner thighs, getting closer and closer to the apex with each pass.

I cry out when he suddenly rubs the end of the handle against my clit through my panties, my whole body aching for him. I move my hips with him, unashamed with how turned on I am and how much I want him.

"That's my girl. That's it, Katarina. Take what you want." Dante kisses me long and hard, his tongue sweeping into my mouth to tangle with mine. I slide my fingers through his hair, pulling at the roots. He groans, the vibrations traveling though me like the deep rumble of thunder.

Before the kiss can lead to more, though, he steps back, no longer touching me. "No!" I protest, and he shakes his head.

"Stay right there, babygirl. Stay right there and remember that you trust me." I nod my head. "Good girl."

Dante doesn't go as far away as he did with the other

target. He stands there for a moment, eyes roaming over my half-exposed body. I'm too wound up to even remember to be afraid. That is until he picks up a knife and throws it, landing to the left of my head.

"Grab it," he instructs.

My chest heaves, my breathing labored, but I reach up and hold onto the handle protruding from the target above me.

He picks up another knife, and this time I'm more aware of his actions as the lust-fueled haze dissipates and I realize that he's throwing knives at my head.

I start to panic, feeling like I'm not getting enough air into my lungs.

"Breathe, babygirl," he soothes. "Just breathe."

I look into his eyes and take a deep breath, and he throws the next knife. I pinch my eyes closed automatically, and this one lands above the other side of my head.

"Grab that one, too." I do as he says and he throws the next knife lower this time, hitting the target right beside my inner left thigh. I gasp. "Don't move," he demands, and throws the next knife, this one landing on the inside of my right thigh. "Now you can't close your legs," he taunts, and I test this, trying to move my legs but am blocked by the protruding handles. "Look at me."

My eyes immediately flash up to his. He raises his arm and throws another knife, this one looking like it's going to hit me dead in the face. I pinch my eyes closed at the last millisecond, just as the dull thud of the blade lodges in the target directly above my head.

My heart is about ready to beat right out of my chest and

my head spins, lightheaded from lack of oxygen.

When I'm able to open my eyes again, Dante is standing right in front of me. "You did so good, babygirl. Feel how fast your heart is racing?" I nod my head. "And you still trusted me. So beautiful," he murmurs, dragging the handle of his final knife down the center of my chest and torso. "Keep holding the handles and keep your legs spread. My cock is fucking begging to be inside of you, but I can't fuck you yet."

"Dante…"

"Shh," he hushes, dragging the cool blade up my inner thigh. He rubs the blunt end of the handle against my clit through my panties again, and I whimper. Everything is heightened. My nerves are drawn tight, making every touch feel like the pluck of a guitar string, sending waves through my body.

Pulling my panties to the side, Dante groans. "You're fucking soaked, Katarina. Which means these are pointless now." Sliding the blade beneath the fabric covering my pussy, he twists his wrist and the blade slices right through it. I gasp in surprise, and he repeats the motion over my hip. "I'm keeping these," he declares, inhaling them. "My favorite scent," he groans, shoving the destroyed fabric in his pocket. "How did it feel to be my target?"

"I knew you wouldn't hit me," I whisper, and he begins to rub my clit with his knife's handle again.

I rock my hips with him, mewling like a cat in heat. "That feels so good," I moan, and he slides the end of the handle through my wet folds, circling my entrance.

"I told you there's a fine line between everything,

babygirl." He penetrates me with an inch or two of the handle and my inner muscles tighten around it.

I feel wild, my eyes wide and on his.

What is he doing to me?

He wants to fuck me with the handle of his knife, and I'm inclined to let him. If I can't have him yet, then I want to have a piece of him inside of me. I felt his power in the knife when I held it. It's inside of it — infused in its very design and elemental makeup.

Dante palms my cheek and presses his forehead to mine. "I want you to come all over my knife, Katarina. I'm going to keep this one on me so that any time I have to use it, you're with me. And when I have to clean it of some fucker's blood, that means I'll get to have you come all over it again."

Moaning, I push my chest against his.

He runs his nose down the bridge of mine. "I'm going to make you come so fucking hard all over it."

"Please," I beg, feeling his lips close to mine. "Please."

Dante kisses me, bruising my lips with the force of his as he pushes the knife another inch inside of me.

My hands grip the knife handles above my head to the point of pain and my legs automatically try to close to aide in getting him to stay inside of me, but the handles there are preventing that.

I have to take what he gives me.

I can feel the twisted design of the handle rubbing my walls and I moan, my head falling back against the target with a dull thud as Dante pulls it out and rubs my clit — over and over until I'm dripping. Only then does he reward me with another slow insertion.

He goes slow at first, then picks up speed with short, quick thrusts into me before slowing down again. The sounds coming from me are unlike anything I recognize. I don't have control over anything that's happening or how I'm feeling, and it's completely freeing. Like I'm flying down an empty highway on a motorcycle, unsure if there's a bend in the road up ahead, and unsure how to stop if there is.

He circles my clit and then slides down my drenched folds, past where I need him, and instead rubs at the tight rimmed muscles of my back entrance.

I gasp, then moan as he presses against me there. "This isn't for today, but just know that I'm going to claim every part of you. I want you filled with me in every fucking hole you have. I want you to feel it all."

"Yes," I sigh. "Please."

"That's my good girl," he praises, bending to lick my nipple. Bringing the handle back to my clit, he rubs it in tight circles as he flicks his tongue over my nipples.

My legs start to shake. I can't take much more. "Dante," I moan.

"That's it, babygirl. Now, come all over my knife." He pushes it back inside of me, hilt deep, and sucks on my nipple as hard as he can while pressing down on my clit with his finger.

I lose it.

Crying out, I bite my lip, not knowing if this place is soundproof or not as wave after wave of pleasure rushes through me. I can't stop coming. My inner muscles cling to his knife's handle, wanting more.

"Look what you did for me."

I peel my eyes open to see him holding his knife up, the entire thing coated and dripping in my come. Dante licks up what has fallen on the blade and then puts it right into the waistband of his pants.

"I don't think I'll ever get used to how sexy you look when you come for me. Let me look at you." Dante takes a step back and looks me over from head to toe and back, licking his lips.

He slides his fingers through my pussy and brings them right to his lips, licking them clean. "Why is it you keep getting better with every taste?"

"I don't know," I whisper, and he licks his lips, going back for a second swipe.

Bringing his fingers to my mouth, he paints my lips with my come and my tongue darts out to wipe them clean, catching Dante's finger still lingering on my bottom lip.

"Maybe it's because of you," I tell him, and his eyes fall half-closed, filled with lust. "It used to take a lot to get myself to orgasm. Now I think I could with just the thought of you. You've changed me, Dante. You've made me better for you, and maybe that's what you taste."

Dante grips the side of my neck, commanding my undivided attention. "Let me be clear, babygirl. You better never think that shit again. You tasted like heaven the first time, and you'll always taste like heaven. You *never* have to be better for me. You're fucking perfect exactly as you are. Got it?"

"I didn't mean—"

"I know what you meant," he says, cutting me off. "But I never want you to think anything like that again. You're already too good for me. I know that," he grinds out, his fingers pressing into my flesh. "My hands should never be able to touch you. I'm death, and you're life."

I let his words float over me. This man believes he's not worthy of anything but death. He delivers death like a dealer handing out cards in a poker game. But what he might not know, is that I'm amazing at poker. I'll win him over eventually.

Taking my hands away from the knives above me, I place one on his shoulder and run a finger down his scar with the other. "Tell me about this."

His eyes dart between mine, not answering me right away. "I got it the night your father found me. He brought me into your home a few days later after I was cleaned up and got treated." I continue to pet his scar, and I can see he gets lost in my soft, slow caress. "I was a street kid for about a year. I survived any way I could. It was a quick learning curve, but I wasn't going back to my father, so I found a way. I learned how to fight and steal for whatever I needed."

"You were still so young," I whisper, and he shrugs, as if it was no big deal.

"I pretty much kept to myself, but there was a group of runaways that stuck together. We would lean on each other if we needed it, but we were all loners. We all had our own stories and reasons for being out there that none of us talked about it.

"There was this newer girl, though, who was only out with us for a couple weeks, and she was having a rough time. She was sixteen, but was so neglected and malnourished that she looked like she was no more than thirteen. I heard her screaming for help one night on my way back to our small camp. There was a grown man twice her size and age pushing her against the side of a building, trying to tear her clothes off. I got to her in time and tore the asshole off of her."

"He obviously didn't like that," I say gently, stroking his scar.

"No, he didn't. We fought. He just so happened to have been better with a knife than I was."

"That's when you got this."

"Yes."

"How does my father factor in?"

"Well, he was only good with the knife for so long. I eventually got it from him and killed him. Your father was walking by the alley and saw everything. He came right up to me and gave me two options. Stay and be found by the police and no doubt go to prison for murder since I was a no-good street kid, or go with him and he'd make the body disappear and train me so that I'd never have that"—his eyes dart down to my hand that's caressing his scar—"happen to me again. He promised to give me a purpose in life, and I have one. I protect your family and I'm good at it."

"You're okay with everything he made you do? What Leo makes you do?"

Dante's eyes thunder. "The men I deal with are fucking scum. They deserve everything I do to them."

"I'm sure," I say quickly, the air around us swirling with a cloud of Dante's anger. After a long few seconds, his eyes come back into focus.

"I do it for you," he tells me. "Every man I've tortured for information. Every man I've killed for the family. It's always been for you. One less piece of shit that could hurt you. One less piece of shit that could take you and use you as leverage against your father and brothers so that'd they do exactly as they wanted."

"Dante..." Words fail me as I process what he just said. I've had a dark angel watching out for me and I didn't even know it. He's always been there, purposefully just on the outskirts so I wouldn't know. But if I had known, what would or could I have done? I'm only now just realizing the power I have within me to wield as my own weapon.

"I'm your shadow, Katarina. I'm with you in the light and dark. You shine and I'm right there behind you, blinded by your light. You sit in the dark, and I'm every inch of that darkness, blanketing you so you're not alone. Ever."

"Who watches over you?" I ask, catching him off guard.

"I do," he finally answers, and my heart breaks for him.

Sliding my hands through his hair, I scratch at his scalp, eliciting a low rumble from his chest. "Let me be that for you. Let me be the one who backs you up and protects you."

"I don't need protecting, Katarina."

"I know, but I want to. I want you to be able to rely on me."

"You want me to take you with me when I have to hunt down someone who hasn't paid their debts? Someone who has been skimming from the games he runs for us? Someone who has betrayed the family and turned to another for help in exchange for information on us?"

"Yes," I say confidently. "I just proved to you that I'm a good shot, didn't I?"

"Katarina, I'm not putting you in any position to get hurt

again. You don't need to worry about me."

"You're not getting what I'm saying." I dig my nails into his scalp. "I'm trying to say that I want you to trust me. That you *can* trust me." I swallow the lump forming in my throat from all of the suppressed emotions I'm suddenly feeling. "I want to be needed, Dante. I want you to need me."

His lips crash against mine and I kiss him back just as fervorous, pouring into him just how glad I am that he feels exactly as I do.

Obsessed.

Crazy.

Needy.

Grateful.

And totally and completely out of control with no idea how to deal with it all.

"I need you," he growls against my lips, then kisses me before I have a chance to respond. "You're the only thing that's kept me alive all these years, Katarina. *You.* I've beat my cock off every night wishing I could have you. I never want you to doubt how much I fucking need and want you. But if you need more proof, I'll tell you that I beat that motherfucker you were talking to online to within an inch of his life to never talk to you again. I didn't want you sharing your secrets with him. I didn't want him knowing anything about you that I didn't. I was there when Stefano told Leo that he found your profile, and I told him I'd take care of it. And I fucking did."

"Dante—"

"No," he says sharply. "Your secrets are mine, babygirl. I want to know every single thing about you. I want to know your fears, your dreams, your wants, your needs, your fantasies. Give me everything, Katarina. I want everything."

"What if I want everything in return? It can't be one-sided because you think I can't handle it. I want to know each and every one of your dark secrets, fears, desires, hopes, and dreams, too. That's the only way this can work."

"You want to know every fantasy I have? Every dark and depraved thing I've done?"

"Yes. And more."

"Then tell me a secret. Something I don't know."

"I graduated university a few months ago. With honors."

His eyebrows clash together. "I didn't know that."

"I know. No one did."

"Why not? That's a huge fucking deal. You've worked hard."

"I know. I just... Everyone was dealing with stuff over the past few months and I didn't think celebrating me was appropriate when my brothers were fighting for their women."

"You matter, Katarina," he says fiercely. "You matter," he repeats, letting it sink in. "It's not just your brothers that people respect. Your cousins and our soldiers respect the hell out of you. Did you not see that when we walked through the gym?"

"I did."

"Then you should know that we're here for you when you're suffering and we're here to share in every triumph. Especially graduating college. And with honors? That's fucking amazing, Katarina."

"Thank you," I say softly, and he brushes his fingertips

across my cheek. "Tell me one of yours."

"Everything I've told you so far has been a secret, Katarina. I don't talk about myself."

A small smile turns the corners of my lips up. "That means you have a lot to tell me. I'm just asking for one right now."

I see something flash through his eyes, but then it's gone. "That song you heard me playing last night…it was yours."

"What?" I breathe, my heart twisting.

"It was after your eighteenth birthday party that I started it. I sat down at the piano after watching you all night, smiling and laughing, and it just came out of me. I've added to it over the years with everything I learn and see."

"Dante," I whisper, at a loss for words. "Will you play it for me?"

His tongue swipes across my bottom lip and I open for him. He kisses me long and slow this time, savoring me.

"It's yours," he says against my lips. "I'll play it for you any time you'd like."

"Who taught you how to play?" I ask, and he pulls back, pain slashing his features.

"That's a story for another time."

CHAPTER 15
Dante

"Where the fuck have you been? Why have you been acting off these past few days?" Leo scrutinizes. "Is it Katarina?"

"Why would it be her?"

He levels me with a look. "Because she suddenly seems to be okay with being around you. I heard she disappeared from dinner on Sunday and so did you from our meeting. She demanded to ride alone in the car with you. You sat next to her this morning like her bodyguard. And you showed her around the gym today."

Fuck.

"I'll ask one more time. Is there anything you want to tell

Rebecca Gannon

me?"

I know I need to tell him, and I know if I lie, he'll know, and it'll make it much more likely that he'll kill me before I can make my case. He'll probably kill me anyway, though. So if I'm going to die for touching his sister, then I only wish I hadn't denied her last night so I could die with the memory of being inside of her on my mind. Although, today with the knives... *Fuck me...* She handed her trust over so fucking beautifully.

Leo's sitting behind his desk and I grip the back of the chair in front of me, the leather creaking under the pressure. "Where should I start?"

"How about the beginning."

"Katarina and I..." I shake my head. "We're it, Leo. She's mine."

His jaw ticks. "Excuse me? Since when?"

"Since always. She's the only reason I'm still here. Still alive, I mean. Just thinking about being with her one day has kept me laser focused on every job I've been given. She's not marrying Santino. Over my dead fucking body will she marry him or anyone else."

I can see his mind working overtime. "And what? You're going to marry her?"

"Yes," I answer without hesitation.

Leo lets out a humorless laugh, rubbing his chin. "You know I respect you, Dante. But Katarina...she's my fucking sister. To know that you want her like that..." He shakes his head. "I know the shit you've done, Dante."

"And what about what Santino's done? And you? I know the shit you've done, and yet you get to have Abrianna.

You get to love her."

"You love Katarina?"

Gripping the back of the chair harder, I grind my teeth together, not wanting to have to tell him before I do her. "It's more than that. Love seems too weak of a word to label how I feel and what she means to me."

"How long have you been sneaking around with her behind my back?"

"Since Sunday. Officially."

"And unofficially?"

Leo is the boss for a reason. He knows how to keep his emotions and what he's thinking under tight control so that no one else knows or can gauge which way he's swaying in an argument or conversation.

"We never did anything before Sunday," I tell him. "I'll swear on anything you want. I was waiting for her to be ready."

His jaw flexes.

Taking his phone out, he dials a number and holds it to his ear. "Get down to my office. Now," he clips, then tosses his phone on the table. I don't bother asking who's coming since I'll know soon enough. I've learned to stay quiet, to observe, and to only speak or take action when necessary. It's what's kept me alive this long.

I take a seat to wait, except when it's Katarina that walks through the door, my defenses go up. She looks between Leo and me, and I see the moment she knows what's going on, because her spine straightens and she stands behind the chair beside me, gripping the back of it just as I was.

"Why was I ordered to come down here?" she asks, her

voice strong and solid.

"Maybe you can clear something up for me." Leo leans back in his chair and crosses his arms.

"About?"

"You and Dante."

"What about us?"

"When were you planning on telling me?"

Katarina sighs and throws her hands up. "Why are you being so vague, Leo? Just spit out what you want to ask me and what you need clarity on?"

"You're fucking Dante," he says harshly, as if it's the dirtiest thing she can possibly do in this world.

"Watch your mouth, Leo," I fire back, and he levels me with a deadly glower.

"You watch *your* mouth. Did you forget who you're talking to? I'm the head of this family, and no one, not even my brothers, talks to me like that."

"It seems you forgot you're talking to your sister."

"Alright," Katarina says, trying to break the tension. "First of all, Leo, Dante and I aren't fucking. Not yet, at least," she adds, and Leo's jaw ticks. "He wanted to talk to you before things went any further, even when I tried to sway him otherwise."

"Kat—"

"No," she says firmly. "You brought it up. Rather rudely I might add. So, now I'm going to talk and you're going to listen. I've been kept hidden in that big house like some prize just waiting to be given to someone. First, by father, and then by you. I always knew what was coming for me. Father told me what my duty to the family was. Then he was killed, and I thought perhaps you'd change that path for me, but you didn't. You haven't. You proved that fact over and over, which means I'm the only one who can create the future I want."

"And you want that future to be Dante? What do you even know about him?"

"What I need to know," she defends haughtily. Jesus, she's sexy when she's defending me. And the absolute certainty and sureness in her declaration has my cock stiffening. "What do *you* even know about me, Leo?"

"What are you talking about? You're my sister."

"That doesn't mean you know me. I love you because you're my brother, but I can't say I know you, and you don't know me. We're not that kind of family. We don't sit around and talk about ourselves. If we did, then you'd know that I'm more than just someone who likes to shop. You'd know that I graduated college early a few months ago."

Leo finally shows an emotion other than indignation. "What?"

"Yes. Imagine me, not wanting to tell anyone because I didn't want to take away from what you all had going on in your lives. But why should I have to feel like telling my family I did this great thing is a burden somehow?"

Leo's face falls. "You shouldn't."

"Exactly. And I shouldn't be some kept woman hidden away just waiting for you to tell me where I'll be going next and with whom I'll be spending my life with. I decide that."

She's fucking amazing.

A fucking queen.

I would never ask her to come down from her throne to

slum it with someone who has killed more people than he can remember. But if there's any soul left in me worth saving, it's because of her, and it's for her. And I fully plan on climbing and clawing my way up to her throne from beneath the earth so that she never has to feel like she's settled for the street kid her father brought home as a project.

"You're right."

Katarina raises her chin in victory. "I know."

Leo turns his gaze to me, leveling me with the weight of his power. "If you do anything to hurt her, know that I will personally use everything my father taught us, and even a few things he saved just for me, to make you feel pain like you can't even imagine. Our history and mutual respect will cease to exist or matter if you do anything that puts Katarina in danger."

"I can handle myself," Katarina defends.

Leo shoots her a glare, so I intervene. "She can, Leo. She shoots better than some of our guys."

"How?"

"Does it matter?" Katarina asks.

"Yes."

"I've been going to the range in the back house for a few years. It's fun." She shrugs, and Leo just looks at her in disbelief, as if he doesn't know his sister at all. Which, to be fair, he doesn't. She lets people see what she wants them to, and I respect the hell out of her for that. I'm the exact same way. No one knows anything about me unless I want them to, and I never want them to. You can't have anything used against you if you're only seen as a ruthless killer with nothing and no one they care about.

That's the only downside to claiming Katarina.

She's always been my single weakness.

But even if everyone knows, I know I can protect her. And I'll teach her to protect herself, too. She's not going to be some helpless housewife, and I'd never want her to be. I know she doesn't want that either.

"You protected her by keeping her locked away. Your father, and now you, thought that was the best decision and the best way, but it's not. Katarina is one of you. She's strong, resilient, and fucking lethal. I know you just think of her as your sister and someone to protect, baby, and handle with kid gloves, but she doesn't want that. And while I know she's fully capable of telling you all of this herself, I'm fucking telling you so I know you're listening.

"She's going to do whatever she wants and I'm going to protect her above all else. I'd lay my life down for her without hesitation. I've always been willing to do that. I wouldn't even have to think twice."

I reach out and rub the back of her thigh beside me. "Katarina's a Carfano. She's not weak. Whatever she wants, I'll give her. Just as I know you wouldn't deny Abrianna a single thing she wants, I'm not going to deny Katarina a single thing. She will have everything, and then some. She's the only reason I'm still breathing, and she'll always only be that reason."

Leo stares at me, his face made of stone.

One, two, three seconds pass in silence, letting my declaration sink in. When he stands, I do the same, and he rounds the table to stand before me.

We're the same height.

Eye-to-eye. Nose-to-nose. Toe-to-toe.

The air between us is tense until he holds his hand out. I look down at it, relief I didn't think I'd feel flooding through me at his approval. Leo doesn't offer second chances when it comes to his family, and with the firm shake I give him, his grip tightens, letting me know without words that he'll destroy me if I fuck up.

But I'd destroy myself before he could if I were to ever fuck up.

CHAPTER 16
Katarina

Taking a sip of coffee, I rest my elbows on the counter and close my eyes, the hot liquid giving me a burst of life. Leo surprised me. He shook Dante's hand. He shook his hand in a silent acceptance of us.

Of course, I was told they had business to discuss and the others were coming down, so I came back up here to my apartment, unsure of what came next. But what was supposed to just be some business to discuss, turned into an all-night thing, and I had to spend my night alone when all I wanted was Dante.

He doesn't have to hold back from me anymore, but of course family business comes before my need to have him make me his.

I know there's still the attempt on all of our lives, but there's always going to be a threat waiting around the next corner. What matters is if I'm ready for it. If I'm prepared. I want to be a force all on my own, not just someone that needs protecting.

Downing the rest of my coffee, I call Abrianna. "Hey, Kat, how are you today?"

"Good. I was just wondering if you wanted to head down to the gym and see if we can get any of the guys to teach us some self-defense? I want to be prepared for anything."

"What about your leg?"

"I'll be fine. I just won't do anything crazy."

"Well, you're in luck. Leo taught me a few things these past couple months and I haven't practiced them in a while. Should I invite Angela? Tessa had to go back to Atlantic City for rehearsal."

"Oh, too bad. But yes, invite Angela. I think it'll be good for us all to know a few moves."

"Exactly. I'll come down to get you in a half hour?"

"Sounds good."

We hang up and I brew myself another cup of coffee while I wait for her. I take my hair out of its French braids and re-do them so it's out of my way. I still can't take a shower or bath until tonight, so I was forced to wash my hair bent over the tub last night and to clean myself with a washcloth again. It's seriously a hassle and I can't wait to feel the hot stream of water from a shower again or soak in a bath with essential oils.

I slip my phone in the pocket of my sweatpants just as there's a knock at the door. "Hey," I greet, opening it and smiling at the two of them.

"Ready to go kick ass?" Abri asks, punching the air between us.

"Yes," I say with a laugh, and Angela shakes her head, smiling.

"Luca thinks he's all the protection I need, but I still want to know how to defend myself."

Abri rolls her eyes. "Typical man. But we can't always rely on them. They can't be by our sides 24/7, nor do we want them to be. And it's not even about having to use what we learn. It's the power of knowing that you *can* defend yourself if necessary. No one actually hopes to fight for their life."

"Precisely." I nod, and Angela flinches, wrapping her arms around her middle. It makes me wonder for the hundredth time what she's been through. But that's not my story to pry into.

"So, did you tell Luca you were doing this with us?"

"No, he's busy with something. I just texted him saying I was going to be with you two. I figured I could surprise him later. He didn't even come home last night."

"Neither did Dante," I add, and both sets of eyes zero in on me like lasers.

"And how do you know that?" Abri asks me pointedly.

"Oh…uhm…" I go to tuck my hair behind my ear but remember it's in braids. "We told Leo yesterday about us."

"You did?"

"Yeah. Some very unpleasant words were exchanged,

but after Dante convinced Leo we were it for each other, they shook hands. In man terms, Leo gave us his blessing, even though I wasn't going to accept anything less."

"I'm really happy for you, Kat." Abri smiles, pulling me in for a hug. "Can I tell you something, though? The first time I met Dante, I knew to be afraid of him. There's something about him that's just…"

"Lethal?" Angela finishes, and Abri nods.

"Exactly."

"Luca had him come and get me when I had to go to see my brothers again, and I was terrified just looking at him."

"He has that effect on people," I tell them, loving that I see something in him and know him in a way that no one else does.

Getting down to the gym, there's five or six guys in and around the MMA cage, and another is lifting weights. But no one is over by the mats, which is where the three of us go. A few of the guys turn to look at us, surprise written all over their faces at seeing the three of us down here. They quickly cover it up, though, and go back to yelling at the two men fighting in the cage.

"Alright," Abri starts, stretching her arms out. "I told Leo I didn't want to be helpless, so he's taught me a few moves. One is for if someone grabs me from behind in a chokehold, and the other is for if someone comes from the side and grabs my arm."

Abrianna proceeds to teach us how to get out of the two holds, and luckily neither do anything to irritate my leg.

"You ladies need some help?" one of the guys that was around the cage comes up and asks us.

"Abrianna is just teaching us some moves in light of what happened. We want to be prepared."

"I can help you out. You can practice on me." He flashes us a charming smile. "You don't have to be gentle when you fight me off."

"And your name is?" I ask.

"Carlo."

"Well, Carlo, I'm–"

"I know who you are, Katarina." He winks. "I'm sorry to hear you got hurt."

"Thank you. It was just a graze, though. I'll be fine."

"Can I help you three out? I can even teach you a few new moves if you're interested."

"Sure, why not?"

I look away, but I can feel his eyes on me. He knows better than to flirt with or look at Abri and Angela, but Dante and I are still unknown. Otherwise, I know he wouldn't be flirting with me right now.

"Who wants to go first?"

"I will," Abri volunteers. "Did you see what we were doing earlier?"

"Yeah. Ready?" Abri nods and he stalks around her to come at her from behind, wrapping his arm around her neck and dragging her backwards.

I notice he's careful where he puts his hands and how much pressure he's putting on her, but that doesn't mean Abri goes light on him, too. She turns her head opposite the direction of his elbow and sweeps her leg out to stop him from going any further. She bends at the waist and jabs her elbow into his lower abdomen, which has him distracted

139

enough for her to slip away.

"Yes!" she cheers, clapping once. "I did it!"

"Alright, let me try," Angela says.

We all manage to get free on the first try, and then Carlo goes through helping us with disarming an attack from the side when your arm is grabbed.

"Want me to show you how to evade an attack from straight on? What if you find yourself cornered with someone coming straight at you?"

"Shoot them," I say simply, and they all look at me. "What?"

"Nothing." Carlo grins. "You could do that, yes. But let's just say for this scenario, you don't have a gun."

"Alright, what should we do?"

Carlo goes through showing us how to deflect an arm grab by grabbing theirs first and turning to elbow them in the groin. Abri and Angela go first again while I observe to figure out how I want to go about it.

When it's my turn, Carlo smiles down at me. "You don't have to be gentle trying to get away from me."

"Don't worry, I won't be." I turn to the girls and they're all hiding their own smiles, knowing exactly what Carlo is doing.

He comes at me and I try my best to grab him and turn, but my leg bangs against his and I yelp, pain shooting up my leg.

"Get your fucking hands off her," Dante's deep voice commands, and the hands are dropped from me immediately. The entire gym is suddenly quiet as Dante storms towards us, his face thunderous and his eyes on Carlo.

"Hey, man, we were just practicing," Carlo says, raising his hands. But Dante doesn't care, and he punches him square in the jaw. Carlo stumbles back from the force, but Dante doesn't let up. He punches him again and again until he falls to the mats.

Squatting down, he fists Carlo's shirt and pulls him up to say something low in his ear that I don't catch, and then pushes him away.

"Let's go, Katarina."

"Dante, he was just teaching us—"

"Let's go," he grinds out, not letting me finish. And when I don't move, he growls like an angry beast and bends down, grabbing me and lifting me over his shoulder.

"Dante!"

"You weren't quick enough."

Dante carries me out of there for everyone to see, and only when we're alone in the elevator does he slide me down the front of his body until my feet are back on the floor.

"That wasn't necessary. He was just helping us."

"His hands were all over you"

"That's how you teach someone self-defense."

"You cried out in pain."

"What did you say to him?"

"I told him not to fucking touch you ever again. I told him you're mine and under my protection, and to spread the word. Now everyone will know. You have a problem with that, babygirl?"

His possessiveness has my stomach knotting and my core throbbing. "No, I don't."

"Good." Grabbing my face in his hands, he slams his

mouth down on mine, his tongue sliding against the seam of my lips, demanding entrance that I grant eagerly.

I'm so lost in our kiss, I don't even realize we've reached our floor until Dante slides his hands down my back to grip my ass and lifts me up. I wrap my legs around him and tear my lips away as he stalks down the hall, trying to catch my breath.

I bury my face in his neck, inhaling his scent that has my head spinning, wishing I could bottle it up and spray it on everything I own. Licking the column of his neck, I feel the end of his scar on his jaw and follow it up, then pepper it with kisses back down, making Dante grunt.

At his door, he pulls back to look me in the eyes. "I won't be able to stop this time, Katarina. And I can't be gentle with you even knowing it's your first time."

"I know."

"I don't think you do. Because I can barely control myself as it is, and I sure as fuck can't hold back with you in my bed."

Gripping his shoulders, my eyes dart between his. "I don't want you to think about what you think I need. I want you to take all of my firsts, Dante, and I want you to do it exactly how you've always wanted to. No holding back. I want to feel it all with you. Pain, pleasure, and everything in between."

CHAPTER 17
Dante

Fuck. Me.

I capture her lips again and she wraps her arms around my neck, smashing her chest against mine.

Devouring her mouth, I plunge inside with my tongue and she moans, giving me complete access. I sweep around, tangling with hers in a kiss that isn't anything short of messy and full of need to get as close as possible.

I pull away long enough to open my door and kick it closed, barely able to make it down the hall and into my room without just laying her down on the fucking floor.

Tossing Katarina on the bed, I rip her shirt off and unclasp her bra, throwing it to the floor. Her tits are fucking perfect, and her dark, dusty rose nipples are pebbled tight and pointing right up at me.

I reach out and cup them in my hands, her resound groan music to my ears. Taking her left nipple in my mouth, I roll it between my lips and suck hard. I swear she tastes like fucking honey, spiked with something more to get me addicted.

"Dante," she moans, my name dragged from the depths of her soul — calling to me.

"You're delicious, babygirl," I murmur into her skin.

"Please," she begs.

"Please, what?"

"I don't...I don't know," she pants, her quick breaths sending her tits into my face.

"All in time, Katarina," I placate, moving over to pay her other nipple equal attention, making her cry out.

My girl doesn't know what it feels like to be licked, sucked, and kissed over every inch of her, and the possessive devil in me is screaming, MINE. He's screaming to claim her. He's screaming to take care of her every need and desire. He's screaming to come out and play, and show her exactly who he is to find out if she can handle him.

Kissing my way down her stomach, I start to pull her sweatpants and panties down, kissing her hips as I go. I drag my mouth down the tops of her thighs and scrape my teeth over her knees, making her legs quiver and spread for me.

So beautiful.

So responsive.

I ease her pants and panties over her bandages, not wanting to cause her any pain. At least, not that kind of pain.

I'm still fucking angry that she's hurt at all, but right now, in this moment, I push it away so I can give her exactly what she needs.

Standing at the foot of the bed, I look down at Katarina and take in every inch of her as she's laid out for me like the fucking treasure she is. She's absolutely beautiful. Her hair is fanned out around her head, her skin is flushed, her lips are swollen from my mouth, her nipples are red and taut from my fingers and mouth, and her pussy is pink, swollen, and glistening with her need for me.

For me.

Dante Salerno.

The goddamn executioner.

A fucking murderer. A savage. A street kid who was taken in by a mob boss who turned me into the killer I am.

I've killed who's needed killing and I've beaten men half to death who've needed a lesson in paying their debts. I'm everything this world fears will come for them if they step out of line, and yet this woman before me is eager for me to touch her in every possible way and fill her with my cock until she's screaming my name and I'm forever imprinted inside of her.

"My beautiful Katarina," I mutter, rubbing my jaw. "I've waited years to have you. Do you know that?" She nods, but I shake my head. "No, you don't know. I've had other women, trying to distract myself from how much I wanted you when you weren't mine to want. But when your father told me I wasn't allowed to want you, I decided right then and there I wouldn't be with anyone else until I had you."

"My father knew?" she asks, her eyes wide.

"He saw the way I was looking at you and told me I wasn't allowed to have you. Ever."

"When?"

"You were seventeen."

"You haven't been with a woman since? That was five years ago."

"I know how long it's been, babygirl." I rub my dick through my pants, aching to be inside of her. "I've spent every night imagining being with you, and every night with my hand wrapped around my dick trying to ease the pain."

"Pain?"

"Yes, pain. Not being with you has been painful, Katarina."

"I didn't think you felt pain," she whispers.

"Only when it concerns you. I've been shot, stabbed, burned, beaten, you name it and I've experienced it. I could take it and barely notice the pain. But when it comes to you, Katarina, I feel everything. Too much."

She sucks in a sharp breath, her cheeks and neck flushing a pretty pink. "Dante," she sighs, sliding her hands up and down her inner thighs. "I need you. Now."

I'm unbuttoning my shirt, and Katarina's eyes eat up every inch of chest and stomach I expose. And when I push it off my shoulders, her eyes flare and she licks her lips, making my cock jump at her approval.

My girl likes what she sees and I fucking love that. Having her look at me like I'm something she wants to taste is a miracle. From the devil or God, I don't know, but either way, I'll let her do whatever she wants with me.

Her eyes zero in on my hands as I slip the button of my

pants free and slide the zipper down, the eagerness written all over her face letting me know my girl is going to give as much as she gets. I don't want to 'teach' her anything. I want her to figure out what she likes and what she wants to do, and let her do it. I'll love every fucking second of it because she'll be so lost in herself and us that I know it'll be an entirely new experience. An otherworldly experience.

My pants fall to the floor and then my boxers, finally freeing myself. I watch her pretty pink pussy glisten as her eyes take in my cock, hard as fucking steel under her gaze.

Scraping my teeth over my lower lip, the mattress dips as I place one knee on the bed, then my other. I grip her shins and spread her open wider for me, my cock pointing straight at where he wants to go.

"I'm not wearing a condom, Katarina. I don't even have any. Haven't needed them. But I don't want anything between us. Not now. Not ever. If you want to go on the pill tomorrow, I'll call the doctor to come and bring you what you need. You can decide right now if you want to stop and I will. I'll stay right here and jack off with you beneath me so I can come all over your tits. It's your choice, babygirl."

Katarina's chest rises and falls with her labored breaths, her eyes glassy as she licks her lips, turned on by my words. I fucking love this look on her.

I don't want her to tell me to stop, but I will if it's what she wants. Just the thought of filling her with my come and the possibility of getting her pregnant has the primal beast in me pounding his chest.

I want her tied to me.

I want a part of me to always be with her if anything

happens to me.

"I want you inside of me, Dante. Nothing separating us. But I'm also going to call the doctor tomorrow. I want to enjoy you without worry for a while."

A while. I can give her that. But not too long.

"I can give you both." Aligning myself at her entrance, her neck arches back and she pinches her eyes closed. "No. Open your eyes. I want to see how you look when I'm filling you with my cock. I want to see the moment I take your virginity and make you mine."

Her breath catches and she does as I say, her eyes holding mine with an intensity and determination to give me exactly what I want.

A true fucking goddess.

A queen.

I can feel her heat and I can't hold back any longer. I push my swollen head inside of her, and because she's so wet, I'm able to slip in with ease.

I groan, my patience and restraint already hanging by a frayed thread, and now she's strangling me with just my tip inside of her. "Fuck, babygirl. You're so fucking wet and hot and tight. I know I'm not going to last long. I've waited too long."

"We don't just have this one time, Dante. I don't care how long you last. I just need you to make this ache go away. Then we can do it all over again, can't we?"

"Oh, I plan on fucking you forever, babygirl." I kiss her hard, pressing her deep into my bed. Just the thought of having forever to do all the things that I want to do to her makes my cock throb.

I push inside another inch and her hot tunnel opens for me, fluttering and then squeezing me. Biting her lips, I pull back to look into her eyes. "Are you ready? It might hurt."

A smile ghosts her lips. "Good."

Growling, I push forward and she cries out, her nails digging into my flesh as she grips my biceps.

Fuck, my baby wants the pain. She really was made for me.

With no self-control left, I thrust all the way inside of her, and she cries out again, louder this time with her eyes watering. Tears leak out of the corner of her eyes and I lick them away, their salty taste my fuel.

I give her a moment to adjust, sweat beading on my forehead from the effort of holding back as her mouth opens and closes, words failing her. But when she lifts her hips up, silently asking me to move, with her eyes begging me to do the same, I pull out slowly, her pussy clutching me like she doesn't want me to leave her.

Pushing back in slowly, she bites her lip, a suppressed moan finding its way out.

"Let me hear you," I grind out. "I told you already you don't have to be quiet in here." I lick her lips and she releases her bottom one from between her teeth. "In fact, I want you to make me deaf with your screams. It means I'm fucking you exactly how you need to be fucked."

With my cock filling her, I rub her clit and she cries out. "That's it, babygirl, let me know how I make you feel." Swirling my tongue around her ear, I bite down on her lobe and she groans, the rough sound giving me new life and another note for her song.

I want her to give me all of her, always.

I want her to know I'll keep her pieces safe and protect them with my life.

I'm going to keep her whole.

Slowly pulling out of her, I let her feel every inch of me, and the cool air of my room hits my soaked cock, sending a bolt of lightning down my spine.

"I can't go slow anymore," I tell her, dragging my lips across her jaw. "I can't give you any more time to adjust to me." I kiss the side of her mouth. "I can't go easy on you anymore."

"Don't," she pants, her wild honey eyes on fire. Katarina's nails dig into me further and I take the small bite of pain as more fuel.

What my girl wants, she gets.

Thrusting into her, her pussy fucking clings to me like a lifeline. I do it again. And again. And again. I stake my claim as the first and last to ever be inside of this heaven. Or hell, depending on how you look at it. Because while her pussy is taking me towards the fucking light and making me believe in God again, it's also going to rule over me and dictate me like the devil when he has your soul. And Katarina Carfano has my soul.

Her breathing is rapid and uneven. "Dante…I need…"

She doesn't finish her thought, but I don't need her to. "I know what you need." Sliding my hands down her body, she claws at my arms and then the comforter around her while I grip her ass, lifting her up to a new angle.

"Ohmygod," she says in a rush, her head turning to the side as she pinches her eyes closed.

"Look at me," I demand, the tips of my fingers digging into her delicate flesh, hoping I leave my prints on her.

Her eyes peel open and find mine again, and I swear I see the meaning of life in them. The reason for living. *My reason for living.*

I spike into her, needing to fill her with my life so she knows that it's hers.

Katarina gasps with every hit home, until those gasps turn to little cries. I hold her up with one hand and rub my thumb against her clit. She completely loses it. Her fists grasp the comforter and her beautiful skin flushes a deep pink color that matches her pussy.

I slam into her one final time and swirl my thumb around her already sensitive clit, making her scream. Her pussy spasms and clenches around me, taking me deep inside of her, milking my cock and pulling my orgasm from me.

Every part of me is on fire as I spill into her, finding relief for the first time in years. I come so fucking hard I see stars dance around her beautiful face and I swoop down to capture her lips, wanting to taste those stars on my tongue.

CHAPTER 18
Dante

Katarina's on her side, facing me, and I watch her while she sleeps.

I could look at her all day and night and never get tired of the view. I find something new to focus on every time I do. Like now, there's three beauty marks on her shoulder that are the beginning of a connect-the-dots puzzle, leaving me to wonder how many she has on her body and how many shapes and pictures I can create.

I can't sleep with her next to me. Not yet. My mind keeps replaying every second of being with her, and I'm ready to have her again. But not yet. It's only been a half hour, and I want her to rest a little while longer before I take her again.

I slip from the bed soundlessly and walk to the kitchen for a glass of water. Leaning against the edge of the counter, my fingers drum on my leg, notes stringing together in my head to go along with the memory of fucking my girl.

The compulsion is too strong. I have to hear it for myself, not just in my head.

I close the door of the room I have my piano in and sit at the bench, my fingers sliding against the cool wood of the fallboard before opening it slowly. Each time I reveal the keys, it's like I'm giving a small nod to my mother. I respect the sanctum of the playing space. She always told me that knowing how to create music was a gift. All we had to do was press our fingers to the keys and we had the power to change people. To make them feel things they've never felt before.

That's how she got me to practice. I wanted to move her. I wanted to make her proud.

I don't think she'd be proud of me now, after everything I've done. But I still play, and I know she'd like that.

Dusting my fingers over the keys, I close my eyes and see my beautiful Katarina in front of me — hearing the sounds leaving her perfect pouty lips and the look of pure fucking ecstasy on her face as she came.

I start her song that has been forever imprinted in my mind. I keep my eyes closed, my fingers knowing the notes and keys without having to look down. Her song fills the room, my lungs expanding to take it all in as if it's a living and breathing thing to be consumed. And in a way, it is.

I'm almost at the part where I'm going to add more notes to her story when I suddenly feel eyes on me. I turn my head and find my muse standing in the doorway, her body now covered by my dress shirt.

I stop playing and turn myself towards her fully, her eyes going straight for my dick that's ready for her again. I'm not covering up in front of her. I like the feel of her eyes on me too much and the look that comes over her face when she's taking me in.

"Take that off and come here. I don't want you covered. I've gone too long not being able to see you."

Katarina unbuttons the two she had done in the middle and shrugs it from her shoulders, letting it pool at her feet. Her long legs bring her closer to me, and when she's within reach, I stand, wrapping my arms around her waist and kissing her until she's squirming against me.

"Did I wake you?"

"I don't mind," Katarina says softly. "I want to listen to you play. Was that my song?"

"Yes, but I didn't get to finish." Gripping her ass, I lift her up and place her on top of my piano. "Put your feet up. I want to look at you while I play."

Leaning back on her hands, Katarina plants her feet on top of the piano, her perfect pussy open and right in my sightline when I sit back down.

I lick my lips and rub my jaw, wanting to touch her and taste her again, but also wanting to make her a little crazy first. I want her to *hear* how I see her. How I've always seen her.

I start from the beginning again and keep my eyes on her pussy. It flushes even pinker and darker, and her little pearl swells from under its hood. My fingers continue to play her song, flying through the notes in a blur.

Sighing, Katarina's legs open a fraction more and her hips rise off the piano, her pussy growing wetter and wetter. It's a fucking sight to see, and one I'll keep in a safe place in my head to always have.

Fuck, she's beautiful.

My mind is replaying every encounter I've ever had with her through this song, and when I get to today, and being inside of her for the first time, I let myself feel it all, all over again. And I think she knows, because her pussy contracts, wanting me inside of her again.

She's leaking.

Come is leaking from her from me playing her song for her, and I need that heavenly elixir permanently woven into this moment.

My left hand keeps on playing and I reach out to swipe my right fingers through her drenched core. Katarina moans my name and lifts her hips, chasing my touch. I swipe through her with my left hand next and go back to playing the with both hands, letting my fingers spread her come over every key I touch.

I want her essence seeped into the keys that I play for her.

"You're going to come for me, babygirl. Touch yourself."

Her hand immediately goes to her center and she moans, rubbing her clit.

"That's right. Let me see you fuck yourself. Put your fingers where you want mine."

Katarina's slender fingers continue to circle her clit, spreading her legs wider and lifting her hips into her touch, lost in her own pleasure. I let her have control of herself and I don't direct her, even though all I want is to see her fingers disappear inside her tight little hole that's leaking her sweet cream and pooling on my piano.

She rewards me for my patience by sliding her fingers down towards her entrance, groaning when she discovers how wet she is.

I lick my lips, the deep notes pounding through me and vibrating the entire piano so Katarina can both feel and hear my music.

I lean forward, ensnared by the vision before me.

Finally, she slowly inserts her middle finger, and I watch it disappear inside the tight silken tunnel I can't wait to be buried in again. Katarina's moans and mewls add to the crescendo of notes filling the room, along with her scent. She's all around me.

Every part of her is filling each of my senses, making my cock rock-fucking-solid, and I need her to go faster. I need her to finish so I can stuff the hole she currently has filled with just a single slender finger with my cock, stretching her wide.

I groan, that image making my dick leak with pre-come.

Katarina pumps her finger in and out, then rubs her clit with the knuckle of her thumb. Her deep, raw groan matches the music, and her entire body shudders under her touch. She keeps up the rhythm and I play faster, matching her movements. We're both racing towards her orgasm, chasing the finish line.

"Dante, Dante, Dante," she chants, making my chest lurch knowing I'm the one she's doing this for. I'm the one she's thinking of.

Her hips begin moving up to meet her finger, fucking herself like a goddamn goddess. I watch her pussy squeeze her finger, trying to suck it inside to go deeper.

"Please," she cries out, and for the first time, my eyes flash up to hers, seeing the desperation in them.

"Come for me, Katarina. Let me see you fall apart to my song for you. Watch me watch you explode, babygirl."

Her eyes ignite and she bites her lip, my eyes dropping down to her pussy to see her pump herself faster, my words having their desired effect.

"Now," I growl, and her hips fly up to take her entire finger while she presses down on her clit. Katarina screams, and the arm that was still holding her up gives out. She collapses onto her back and I pound out the last bar of notes, my entire body wound tighter than the damn strings of the piano my girl is laid out on.

I need her. Now.

I'm going to fulfill another fantasy I've had rolling around my head for years.

Using the bench as a step stool, I grip Katarina's ankles and push her back to make room for me. I climb on top of my grand piano with her and wrap her legs around my waist, aligning myself at her entrance straight away.

Katarina's honey eyes fly open to meet mine just as I thrust into her, fully sheathing myself in her tight, wet heat.

"Fuck," I grunt, stilling my movements to feel her squeeze me over and over. And when I can't wait any longer, I fuck her — hard and fast.

My hands grip her hips to keep up my pace, and while

she searches for something to hold on to for my unrelenting pace, I watch her tits bounce and sway, her nipples so fucking inviting.

"Play with your tits, babygirl. Pinch those pretty nipples to get yourself there faster."

She obeys me with such ease, crying out when she rubs her taut nipples between her fingers. Her pussy flutters around me, and I feel a rush of wetness between us, making the sound of us fucking, too fucking good. It's messy, and the wet slapping sounds of our bodies joining is driving me damn near insane.

Fire takes root in my scalp and travels down my spine, my cock swelling and my balls heavy.

Katarina starts to flutter around me and I grunt, stuck in the spot of wanting to fill her with my come and wanting to keep fucking her forever. My need to come wins out and I pump into her two more times before the fire takes over and I still inside of her, my roar loud even to my ears as I come harder than I ever have before.

Katarina screams, her back arching off the piano and her neck bending backwards as she milks my cock for everything I have.

CHAPTER 19
Katarina

I can't move.

My legs and arms are heavy, and all I have the energy for is breathing.

It felt as if my soul left my body and touched Dante's before being forced back inside of me and dragged under a thick blanket of calm and quiet ease.

Dante has me draped over him, still on top of his piano.

He played me my song...

It's beautiful. Dark and haunting at some parts, and then soft and light during others. And hearing it while I was spread open before him, his eyes focused between my legs...

I was completely driven by his gaze and the music that

vibrated through me and in the air all around me.

Dante's arm is wrapped around me now, and the steady beat of his heart beneath me is just another reminder that he's really here with me. He's real. This is real.

I doze off to the music of his heart and then come to, I don't know how much later, in the same exact position, content to stay like this with him.

I brush my fingers back and forth across his chest, over uneven circles of raised skin. "What are these from?" I ask softly, knowing he's awake too.

"My father burned me with the butt of his cigarette when I was ten."

"Dante," I breathe, and he begins to stroke my back.

"My mom died that year and my dad didn't know how to handle me. She had ovarian cancer, but by the time it was found, it was too late. She was the only safe place I had. I was a quiet kid who never had friends, but my mom understood me." My heart twists, feeling the pain seeping out of him. "She was a piano teacher at a charter school here in the city and taught me how to play every day after school, starting when I was six, I think. Music connected us. She showed me how to use it to communicate how I was feeling."

I plant a soft kiss to his chest, loving my song even more now. It's a culmination and compilation of everything he couldn't say to me over the years.

"I didn't play a single note after she died. I couldn't bring myself to sit down and play anything at all. And a few weeks later, my dad sold the piano. He was always an asshole. He would drink and throw my mom around, and I would put my headphones on and turn my music up until I couldn't hear anything while I hid like a coward until it was all over."

"You were just a kid, Dante. You couldn't stop him. I'm sure your mom wanted you hidden and safe." Hearing him speak about his childhood makes me wish I wasn't so terrified of him when I was younger. At thirteen, he was still just a kid himself, needing a parent and needing someone to care about him again. What he got was my father. A man who was neither a good parent or caring to, or about, anyone but himself.

"I should've done something," he says, anger still laced in his voice all these years later. "And it took me a while, but I eventually did do something. When she was alive, my dad at least had some good days. That's what made everything seem like it would be okay. But after, all he did was drink, chain smoke, and wish I wasn't in his way or his responsibility to raise on his own. The more he drank, the angrier he got, and the more he saw me as the bane of his existence. That meant I had to be punished and put in my place. Which was down on the ground, beaten into silence and until I couldn't move."

My heart is breaking for him.

I never knew. I never imagined...

"He knew to never hit my face, but I was covered in bruises to the point I would be wearing long sleeves and pants all year long. I didn't like attention, and I didn't want attention. He took me to the ER a few times when it was obvious that my wrist was broken or when he had broken and bruised my ribs so badly, it hurt to breathe or move an inch. The nurses and doctors would ask me about my injuries, but I told them I played a lot of sports. I didn't care enough to tell them the truth. I thought that what was happening was it for me, and I figured I had no one left who cared about me anyhow. Sometimes I'd wish my father just killed me the next time so that I would be set free from the hell I was in."

"No," I say fiercely, wrapping my arm around him, tears falling from my eyes and splashing on his chest.

Dante brushes his fingers across my cheek. "Don't cry, babygirl. Don't waste your tears on something I escaped."

"I can't help it. You were just a kid. You shouldn't have had to go through that. No one should," I croak, my voice thick with pain and sorrow for the little boy who had his mother taken from him and was left with an abusive father who didn't give a shit about him.

No wonder he's always been so closed off and holds himself at a distance from everyone. He hasn't been given a reason to be anything other than that.

"I found a way to live, though," he assures me. "One day I realized I wanted more and I wanted to live, so when I was thirteen, I decided to fight back. I was finally strong enough to take him, and I made sure I won. I made sure he didn't get up from the floor that time."

I rub endless circles against his ribs, soothing both him and myself. "Did you kill him?"

"Yes," he says simply, with no regret in his voice.

"Good," I affirm, and he places two fingers under my chin, lifting my face to look into my eyes. "If he was still alive, I would offer to kill him myself."

Dante's eyes are more open than they've ever been, and they flare with my words. "Thank you. But even if he was still alive, I wouldn't want you to dirty your hands with my past."

"No one knew it was you?"

"I ran away that night and never looked back. I took whatever I could fit in my backpack, any money that was lying around, and the few things left I could pawn or sell that my father hadn't yet."

"Until my father found you."

"Yes. Over another dead body. He offered me a way out with a new last name and life where I wasn't looking over my shoulder, waiting to be caught."

Dante killed two people before he was even old enough to shave. I reach up and stroke the scar on his jaw. "You were helping someone who couldn't fight back. You saved her from someone who didn't deserve to be breathing anymore. I'm glad you killed him, and I'm glad you killed your father. This world didn't need them wasting space anymore."

"You're a little ruthless, aren't you?"

"Yes, when it comes to defending those I care about, I am."

"You care about me," he says — a statement, not a question.

"Of course I do." Swallowing, I find the courage to add, "I more than care about you, Dante."

His whole body stiffens beneath me, and then relaxes, his dark eyes melting into midnight pools that have me ensnared. "Katarina," he starts, my name rolling from his tongue in a smooth caress. Pulling me fully on top of him, Dante slides me up his body so my face is directly above his. "You're my everything, Katarina. I'm going to spend whatever time I have remaining on this earth making sure you always know and feel that. I don't deserve you. No man does. But I need you, Katarina. I love you. I've loved you for so long, it seems as if I've told you a thousand times already."

My heart stops, then takes off double-time, practically pounding out of my chest and into his. Tears well in my eyes again and spill over their rims, falling to Dante's cheeks. "I love you," I whisper, cupping his face in my hands. "You have it wrong, though. I'm the one who doesn't deserve you." Closing the distance, I kiss him until I lose my breath.

Dante kisses my cheeks, my forehead, and my closed eyelids. "I started playing the piano again because of you. You were always on my mind, and the only way I could do something about it and ease the loudness in my head telling me I was a piece of shit who didn't deserve you, was to play. You silence the demons I have riding my back, but you've also created a few new ones. The things I've done…" He pauses, giving a slight shake of his head.

"I don't care what you've done."

"You should. You don't know everything."

"Whatever you've done won't change how I see you or how I feel."

Taking my face in his hands, he kisses me, reminding me again why his past doesn't dictate how I feel.

I lay back down on his chest and trace circles on his ribs, soothing us both into a state of comfort. "What was your name before?" I ask out of curiosity.

"Dante Marini."

"How did you pick Salerno?"

"I read it somewhere or heard it in passing and liked the

way it sounded. I only found out later that it's also a city in Italy."

"It is. I've seen pictures and it looks beautiful. I'd love to go to someday."

"I'll take you. I'll take you anywhere you want to go," he says, and my heart melts. Traveling has been something I've always wanted to do but was always told it wasn't safe for me. But with Dante, I know I'd be safe.

I kiss his chest. "I like Salerno better," I tell him, and his arm tightens around me.

CHAPTER 20
Dante

"Stefano found a trail of Hovan online," Leo tells the room when everyone is seated around the table.

"He's been talking with some of his men through what he believes is a private line." Stefano smirks. "But I got in and found him planning to make a statement at the fight this weekend."

Each month we host an underground, no holds barred, MMA fight night with the exception of one rule – no weapons in the cage or in the crowd. The audience is by invitation only and the fighters represent every crime syndicate in the city as well as a few that come crawling out of the shadows to compete for a hefty purse.

The warehouse location changes every month so we're kept under the radar of authorities, and there's a truce agreement between those walls when anyone enters. There's no business disputes or blood spilled outside of the cage. That's how all five families — Carfano, Antonucci, Melcciona, Capriglione, and Cicariello — are able to be around one another, as well as the Yakuza, Triads, Bratva, Irish, Albanians, and Armenians.

If the truce is broken, then you don't make it out of the warehouse.

Of course, the Cicariellos haven't shown their faces for the past five years, knowing that truce or not, we would kill them for killing Michael and Sal. But since we took them all out, they're no longer a worry.

Now it's Hovan looking to start a war.

"He brought a fighter over from Armenia and plans on taking whoever we enter out."

"And?"

"And he's a big son-of-a-bitch. He's never lost. In fact, he's known for leaving his opponents either dead or crippled."

"Who the fuck has he been fighting?" I ask. "Maybe he doesn't have any competition."

"He will this time," Leo says, looking at me. "He wants to make a statement, then we'll make a louder one. Dante, you're fighting this month."

Is he fucking serious?

My teeth gnash together and my jaw flexes, the gleam in Leo's eyes letting me know this is about more than just winning the fight. This is about Katarina.

He wants to throw me into a cage with a fighter known to kill and cripple? So fucking be it. I'll win, and then I'll go back to my place and fuck Katarina until she's screaming my name.

"Fine," I deadpan, and Leo narrows his eyes, the tension in the room being felt by everyone. "But then we're good."

"What's going on?" Luca asks as Leo and I continue to stare one another down. He raises an eyebrow, challenging me to tell everyone, almost like he thinks I won't do it.

"Katarina won't be marrying Santino because she'll be marrying me," I announce, and feel all six sets of eyes burning holes into me — Leo, Luca, Stefano, Nico, Marco, and Gabriel.

"What the fuck?" Luca growls. "Says who?"

I look them each in the eyes. "Katarina."

"Are you fucking with us?" Gabriel asks.

"When have you ever known me to make a joke, or would think that I would joke about something like this?"

"She wants to marry you?"

"Why? Is that so hard to believe?" I grind out.

"Enough," Leo barks, slamming his fist down on the table. "I've already discussed this with Kat and Dante, and I gave them my blessing. You will fight this weekend," he directs at me, "and it has nothing to do with Kat. You're the best fighter we have."

I nod in agreement, my blood fucking boiling and ready for a fight right now. The men in this room are the closest people I have to family, and now I find myself having to prove my worth to be with Katarina.

I always knew I wasn't good enough for her, but to see it

in their eyes is a fucking punch to the gut.

But Katarina loves me, and she's all that matters. When she told me she loved me, the missing pieces I've felt in me like black voids, slowly sucking the life out of me with each passing day, were suddenly filled, and I was whole again.

She's made me whole again.

"If you don't need me for anything else, I'm going to start training." I walk out of there and head straight for the gym, needing to hit someone.

I always keep spare clothes in the small locker room down here, and after changing, I spend the next two hours challenging everyone around.

I don't hold back, and neither do they. Which is why when I return to my apartment, Katarina looks horrified.

Gasping, she runs to me, raising her hands to touch me, but then curling them into fists at her sides. "What happened?"

"I was training."

"For what?" The fire in her eyes has her honey glowing bright.

"I'm taking the place of our fighter this weekend."

"In what? Why?"

"I'll explain later. Just let me get cleaned up."

"Let me help you. Come on." Taking my hand, she walks me to my bathroom.

"I can do this myself," I tell her. "I usually do."

She pins me with a glare. "I know, but you don't have to. Now, take your shirt off."

"You just want to see me naked, don't you?"

"Just do it," she sighs, putting her hands on her hips.

"You're mad at me?"

"No. Just take your shirt off and let me look at you." Smirking, I do as she wishes, which makes her gasp again. "I'm mad at whoever did this. Who was it?" she growls like a little beast.

"A few guys." I shrug. "It comes with the territory, babygirl. It doesn't hurt that bad. Trust me, I've had worse."

The fire in her eyes diminishes just a little at my last statement, and she runs her hands up my torso. "You have bruises already," she whispers, her touch gentle as she goes over them. "Sit on the edge of the tub and I'll clean your face. I'm assuming you have first aid supplies?"

"In the cabinet under the sink."

Katarina grabs what she needs and kneels in front of me. Carefully, she dabs at a cut above my left eyebrow and one below my right eye with a wet wash cloth, cleaning the dried blood away.

No one's ever cared for me like this before. I usually just shower and put antibiotic cream on any deep cuts to prevent infection. Other than that, I don't care. My body is already covered in scars. What's a few more?

"What are you training for?" she asks carefully.

"Our monthly fight night is this weekend and Hovan plans on being there to watch his guy take ours out, so Leo has me taking his place. I'm the best we have."

She stills, her hand frozen against my eyebrow. "Leo is having you take the spot of a man meant to die?"

"That's not going to happen."

"You don't know that," she says fiercely, the fire back in her eyes. "And neither does Leo. You can't do this, Dante.

I'm not losing you when I've barely gotten to have you."

I cup her face. "Come here."

Bracing herself on my thighs, Katarina lifts herself up and kisses me despite my split lip.

"Let me finish cleaning you up."

"Take a shower with me and I'll let you play doctor all you want."

"I'll take a shower with you if you tell me you won't fight this weekend."

"I can't do that."

"Dante."

"Katarina," I soothe. "I'm going to win. I don't lose."

"You better win," she tells me harshly. "Because if you don't come home to me, I'll go after whoever I have to."

"You keep surprising me, babygirl. But you're sure as fuck not going after anyone without me. I promise I'll come home to you."

"Fine then. Take the rest of your clothes off and get in the shower."

I lift my chin. "You first."

Katarina stands and removes each piece of clothing, tossing them aside until she's completely naked before me.

"You keep getting more beautiful," I muse, rubbing my jaw, and she rewards me with a smile that has me wondering how I've gone this long without it and how I never want to again.

She holds her hand out for me to take, and when I place mine in hers, she pulls it closer to examine my swollen knuckles. "Let me take care of you."

Katarina washes me first, her delicate hands running

over every inch of me. I let her have her moment, and let myself feel cared for for the first time.

I lean back against the cool tiles of my shower and watch Katarina wash herself next, the soap gliding over her soft skin like silk, leaving a soapy trail behind that has my hands flexing, needing to follow that same path.

She doesn't seem to realize she's putting on a show for me, and I only possess so much restraint. Lifting her arms up, she lathers her scalp with shampoo, thrusting her tits out. And when I can't hold back a groan, her eyes find mine and she gives me a slow smile that lets me know she knows exactly what she's doing.

"You teasing me on purpose, babygirl?"

Her smile widens, her eyes darting down to my hand wrapped around my dick. "Maybe."

"If you want me, all you have to do is say so. I am enjoying the show, though."

"That was the idea. But I think I'd much rather have you clean me."

Pushing off the wall, I take us under the spray of hot water and twist my fist in her hair, pulling her head to the side. "Your wish is my command."

Grabbing the bar of soap, I glide it over her arms, back, stomach, and up her chest, circling her nipples. Katarina moans, biting her plump lower lip.

"That's my job," I rasp, and she gasps, releasing her lip just before my mouth covers hers and I bite down where she just was, replacing her teeth marks with my own.

I glide the soap down her stomach and between her legs, sliding it back and forth along her pussy.

Gasping again, she grabs my arms and I delve into her mouth, my tongue clashing and tangling with hers in a slippery kiss that has my cock painfully hard between us. I keep rubbing the soap against her, wanting her to come all over it so that every time I shower, I'm washing myself in her.

I'm well aware that my obsession with her and need to be as close as possible to her has driven me to fucking insanity, but there's no reining it in. There's no taming the mania. And I don't want to.

I rub the bar of soap against her clit and she shudders, moaning into my mouth and letting me feel her love vibrate through me like a low G note.

Backing her up against the tiles, I kiss her harder, deeper, and shove the bar of soap into her greedy pussy. I'm barely able to hold onto it, but when her inner muscles squeeze tight, she pushes it back out into my hand, and I rub her clit until she screams into my mouth. I bite down on her lip, wanting to hear her screams echo off the tiles and marble.

Sweet, sweet music.

I spin us around so she's the one under the water and I rinse the shampoo out of her hair and lather it in conditioner, starting at her ends and then massaging her scalp. Katarina hums her approval, her eyes closed and her face relaxed.

Rinsing the conditioner out, I turn the water off and walk us out of the shower. I wrap her in a big towel and she smiles up at me. "Go sit on the bed so I can finish taking care of your cuts."

"I'm fine, Katarina," I try to tell her, but she just levels me with a glare that's so fucking sexy, I do as she says.

With a smug little expression, she grabs the supplies she left by the tub and crawls up onto the bed next to me. "Turn to face me," she instructs, and I do as she says, loving my girl when she's bossy.

Patting my cuts dry with gauze, she applies antibiotic cream with a Q-tip and then uses butterfly strips to hold my eyebrow cut together. "The one under your eye should be fine to heal on its own. Let me see your hands." I hold them out to her and she shakes her head. The small cuts I got from the glass reopened. "Why weren't you wearing gloves or something?"

"I taped my knuckles. I just threw a lot of punches."

"You do realize I need these hands, right?"

"So do I, babygirl."

"Then you better be careful from now on."

"As you wish," I tell her, and she huffs out a short laugh. "I should probably warn you about something I said to your family today."

She looks at me warily. "What did you say to them?"

"I told them you weren't marrying Santino because you were marrying me." Her hands squeeze mine, shaking slightly as her eyes stay glued to them. "Look at me, babygirl."

Her golden eyes lift to mine and she studies me, her eyes darting between mine. "Why would you tell them that?"

"Because it's the truth."

She shakes her head, pushing my hands away and crawling back on the bed to put distance between us "Dante, you can't say things like that."

"Don't push away from me," I growl, grabbing her legs and pulling her back to me. I lift her onto my lap so she's straddling me and I grip her chin. "Don't push me away."

"Don't tell my family things you don't mean. They don't take things like that lightly. You can't just take it back later on."

"What makes you think I want to take it back? You're not marrying him. You're marrying me."

"Dante—" she starts, then stops, her lips pressed together and her eyes turning glassy. "You can't say that."

"Why not?" I demand, my tone harsher than I intended. "I'm marrying you, Katarina. If you wanted to go right now, I'd wake one of the judges up on our payroll and get him down to City Hall."

"Dante…I…"

"What's got you confused, babygirl? Are you trying to tell me you don't want to be mine?"

"I never said that," she says quickly. "You know I do. I told you that already. I just…marriage has always meant something different to me than other girls. I spent years knowing I had no control over who I was going to marry. My father did. I was going to go to the highest bidder or the one who could give him the most in return. The idea of marriage was abhorrent to me. Then this happened — us — and I…"

"You what?" I urge, needing to know exactly where her head is at.

"I can't even wrap my head around you loving me all these years, Dante. You have no idea…" She shakes her head. "It just seems too good to be true. I'm not someone who gets this lucky."

Pressing my forehead to hers, I close my eyes and take a deep breath, breathing her in. I take her purity and hope it washes away some of my sins, because there's no way in hell she thinks being with me is lucky. There's no fucking way.

"Babygirl." My lips are pulled to hers under gravity's weight. "We're the forever kind of love. The crazed and obsessed kind of love. Don't you feel that?" I ask, my lips brushing hers with every word.

"Yes," she sighs, her lips buzzing against mine.

"Then marry me. You'll come before everything and everyone. That I can promise you, Katarina. You'll want for nothing, and you'll never have to question your place in this world or family, because your place is with me."

Katarina doesn't say anything, and she doesn't have to. I can feel it all. Her arms tighten around me so our chests are crushed together. Her heart is pounding, the beat matching my own.

The magnetic pull is too much.

She closes the distance, kissing me in a way that answers all of my questions, but I still need the words. Pulling back, she tries to chase me with her mouth, but I shake my head. "Is that a yes?"

"Yes," she hisses impatiently, and I growl, taking her lips in a bruising kiss. I rip the towels from our bodies and lay her down, covering her with my weight. I need to be inside of her.

She's already wet and ready for me, and I slide right into my home that's going to be mine for the rest of my life.

CHAPTER 21
Katarina

"I want to go tonight," I tell Dante, and his movements still as he packs his gym bag. The past few days have passed with me seeing Dante only in the evenings when he returns from meetings and training for hours on end. We go through the same ritual of me cleaning his wounds, us showering, and them him giving me the last of his energy as he fucks me until we both pass out.

His eyes slowly raise to mine. "That's not happening."

"Why not?"

"Because the people who are going to be there tonight are not who I want you around."

"I can handle myself."

"I know that, but the vilest men of this city are going to be there tonight, and I can't focus on what needs doing if I know you're there."

"I can't just sit here all night, waiting to find out if you're dead or not, Dante. I can't." I shake my head, crossing my arms over my chest.

"You have to." He grabs my face. "I need to know you're safe. I promise I'll come home to you. Nothing and no one will keep me from that."

"You can't come home to me if you're dead."

"No one's killing me tonight, Katarina. Your father didn't just name me The Executioner because of my job for the family. I used to fight every month for years and I never lost. Not once. I always won, no matter what. Go and hang out with Abrianna and Angela, and before you know it, I'll be back, needing another shower with you." Leaning in, Dante's lips hover over mine as he says, "It's becoming my new favorite routine."

"Me too," I whisper, and he kisses me with fervor, one hand gripping my ass to pull me flush against him, and the other wrapped around the end of my ponytail. "You promise you'll come home to me?" I rasp when he pulls away.

"Always," he promises, kissing me again. "I have something for you," he adds.

"You do?"

Dante walks over to his dresser and pulls open the top drawer, rooting around for something in the back. "No matter how bad things got, I never pawned this. I couldn't. And I guess my dad couldn't either because it was still on their dresser three years after she died. It's the last thing I have of her." Dante holds a little black velvet box in his hand and opens it, revealing a delicate gold necklace with a music note charm. "She said her mom gave it to her when she graduated high school and she never took it off. I hadn't even realized my dad didn't bury her with it until the night I left and found it there. I want you to have it, Katarina. You're the reason I play. You're the reason I have music in my head at all still."

I'm speechless. Tears fall down my cheeks and I swipe them away quickly. "It's beautiful. I'm honored that you'd want me to have this."

Taking it out of the box, I unclasp it and put it around my neck, smoothing my fingers over the two eighth notes charm. "Thank you." Reaching for him, I lift up on my toes and slide my hand through his hair, bringing his lips to mine to give him my love and appreciation.

Dante releases me and I sway where I stand, off-balance. "I'll see you later, babygirl."

I don't have the words or brain capacity to say anything with my head being a fuzzy mess of emotions. And by the time I have it in me to argue about staying here again, he's already gone.

I try, I really do, to keep busy, but I'm in Dante's apartment and all my mind is conjuring are images of him being beaten by some guy who plans on killing him while I'm here doing nothing about it.

I'm not that kind of woman anymore. I'm not meek or

passive anymore.

Moving the charm of my new necklace along its chain, I can't help but think he might have given this to me before he left because he believes there's a chance he won't be coming home to me.

I can't sit here all night and wait.

I pull out my phone and dial the number of someone who I think I can convince to help me. "Hey, Kat, what's going on?"

"Hi, Nico. How's my favorite cousin?"

"Oh, no. What do you want?"

"What makes you think I want something?"

"For starters, you're calling me tonight of all nights. And second, you called me your favorite cousin. You've only ever done that when you've needed something from me that you don't want to go to your brothers for." He's not wrong. I used to use that line on him when I was a teenager and wanted him to take me out for food or ice cream, or just a drive while we listened to music that didn't involve a cavalry following us.

"Fine," I sigh. "You caught me. Are you going to the fight tonight?"

"In a few minutes. Leo and Luca left already, but I had to finish something."

"I need you to take me with you."

The line goes silent, and then a short laugh echoes through. "Not happening, Kat."

"Why not?"

"Because there's no way in hell Leo would want you there. Or Dante. Which is a whole other conversation we need to have. Are you really marrying him?"

"Yes, I am, and I don't care if Leo wants me there or not. I need to be there for Dante."

"No. There's no way I'm bringing you. I'm sorry, Kat, but you don't belong there."

Nico hangs up on me and I throw my phone on the bed, hating that I'm always going to be perceived as someone who shouldn't go here or doesn't belong there because I'm a fucking girl.

This anger in me is new and it's making me erratic, but I don't want to go back to being complacent and *hoping* things will change.

I'm going to change them myself.

Since I decided I was going to go after Dante, the fallout and consequences be damned, something in me seems to have clicked into place. The puzzle pieces that I've always felt have been jammed into the wrong opposing pieces, righted themselves. I woke up and took the power I've always had as Katarina fucking Carfano and embraced it, and I'm not going to suddenly revert back to the Katarina that took orders and let the men in her life make choices for her.

CHAPTER 22
Katarina

Leaving Dante's apartment, I walk down the hall to mine and go straight for my purse, digging around until I find what I'm looking for.

Santino's business card is all the way at the bottom and I pull it out. Under his name, he lists his job title as entrepreneur. Funny.

I never intended on taking this out again, let alone use it to call him, but I have a feeling he's the one person I know won't say no to me.

I know Dante will hate that I'm doing this, but I push that thought away and dial Santino's number before I lose my resolve.

It rings a few times, and then a confused voice answers. "Hello?"

I swallow the lump in my throat. "Santino?"

"Yes?"

"It's Katarina."

"Oh," he says, surprised. "Hi. I wasn't expecting you to call."

"Me either," I tell him honestly, and he laughs.

"What can I do for you?"

"I'm assuming you know about the fights tonight and all the details? Mainly, where it's being held?"

He pauses, clearing his throat. "I do."

"I need you to take me."

"Katarina," he starts, his reluctance ringing clear through the phone.

"I know about your father and how he was the one who set us up at that lunch. I was shot because of him. I could've died."

"I promise I didn't know, Kat," he says quickly.

"I don't need any explanations. If Dante didn't kill you when he did your father, then that's all the confirmation I need that you didn't know. He doesn't give second chances."

"I'm well aware," he clips, clearly not wanting to talk about his father.

"Well, you can earn your trust with Leo if you take me tonight. I need to be there but I don't know where it is or if I need some super-secret password to gain access."

I can hear his smile through the phone. "There's no password. They just have to know you. But Katarina, I doubt Leo knows you're calling me trying to get me to do this, does he? Going behind his back and bringing his sister to an underground fight night doesn't exactly seem like a show of good faith."

"It will because I say it will," I tell him. "I need to be there and you're going to take me. Otherwise, you won't like what I'll have to say to Dante."

"Are you threatening me?" He sounds surprised, and it only makes me madder.

"Yes," I hiss. "Because I'm marrying Dante, not you. And unless you want me to tell him you're no longer needed in any kind of business deal with my family, then you'll meet me on the curb right outside the parking garage of our building in an hour. Is that enough time?"

There's a long pause and I hold my breath. "I'll be there in an hour," he finally says, and I sigh in relief.

"Santino?" I say quickly before he hangs up.

"Yes?"

"Thank you."

"I'm surprised your brothers haven't used you to broker deals before. You're quite effective."

"Thank you. See you in an hour."

Hanging up, my next call is to Abrianna to tell her I have a fashion emergency, and she tells me to come right up.

"Hey, Kat." She smiles, pulling me in for a hug. "What's your fashion emergency?"

"I need a dress for something. Like, right now. I have to be ready in less than an hour."

"Is Dante taking you somewhere nice?" she asks, her whole face lighting up.

"Not exactly. I'm meeting him somewhere."

We walk down the hall to her room and right into her massive walk-in closet. "Okay, so what were you thinking?"

"I was thinking a little black dress." I want to look like I belong, but I don't want to stand out.

"Hmm," she hums, biting her lip as she looks through her hangers.

"I really need to go get my things from the house. I'm sorry I have to ask you."

"It's not a problem. Trust me. I have so many dresses that are too pretty to be stuck in my closet. Ah, here it is." Abri is giddy as she pulls a dress from the rack and holds it out to me.

"Oh, yeah, this is perfect." The little black dress is short, but not too short, with gold chain spaghetti straps and a deep 'v' neckline that's laced-up with a matching gold chain. And when she turns it around, I gasp, the back hanging loose in a scooped cowl neck style.

"Knock him dead." She grins playfully.

"Oh, I think I will." I smile, taking the dress. "I don't want to lie to you, though, and in case Leo comes home angry later, I should tell you that I'm going to the fights tonight."

"What? Why? You want to see men beat each other until one doesn't get up?"

Looking away, worry laces through me that that's going to be Dante. "No, not really. But Leo has Dante fighting tonight and I need to be there."

Abri's face shutters closed. "What do you mean, Leo has him fighting?"

"Dante's been training for days and I'm worried. I know

he's good at what he does, and he's promised me he'll come home, but I still feel like I need to be there. I have this horrible feeling in my gut."

"How are you getting there? Do you know where you're going?"

"That's where I, uh, may get in a little trouble. I called Santino and basically threatened him with the wrath of Dante if he didn't come to pick me up and take me."

"Kat!" she admonishes. "Are you serious?"

"Desperate times calls for desperate measures. I told him I was marrying Dante and not him, so that cleared up any misconceptions of what him escorting me tonight might mean."

"I'm sorry," she sputters. "What the hell did you just say? You're marrying Dante? He asked you to marry him?"

"Well, technically he told everyone he was marrying me before even asking me, but I don't care." I smile.

"It's not too soon?"

"It doesn't feel too soon. We've both waited long enough."

Abri smiles, pulling me in for a hug. "I'm happy you're happy."

"Thank you," I whisper, squeezing her tight. "And I'm really happy you put up with Leo so that you can be in my life too."

"He's not a bad man, Kat," she says softly, pulling away to look at me. "He loves you."

"I know." I nod. "But my family has always made me feel like I'm just a responsibility. Like I'm someone they have to make sure is kept safe and untouched in a little box. But life is about taking chances and getting bumped and bruised along the way to finding yourself. I'm not someone else's responsibility. I'm my own responsibility and am fully capable of making my own choices in life. And if they turn out to be the wrong choices, then so be it." I shrug. "That's how I'll learn and grow. Dante respects that."

"That's fucking beautiful," Abri says in awe, making me laugh.

"Thanks. Now, I would stay, but I have to go get ready. Do you happen to have shoes I can borrow, too?"

"Oh!" she says excitedly. "I have the perfect pair." All of her shoes are displayed openly on shelves, and she eyes it for a second before finding what she's looking for. "I had to buy these when I saw them. I'm obsessed."

"Oh my God," I praise, taking them from her. "They're perfect." They're a four inch black stiletto heel that buckles around the ankle and has gold chains connecting that strap to the one across the toes. "I seriously can't wait to put these on. Expect a picture before I go."

"I will." She smiles. "Now get going so you have enough time. We'll have another girl's night soon."

I smile at the dress and shoes in my hands as I ride back down to my apartment, and after doing my hair and makeup, I slip the dress on over my head and look in the mirror.

Oh, this will do.

I turn to the left and right, loving everything about this dress. It isn't tight, which makes the fact that it's short with a revealing front and back seem more sexy than slutty. The chiffon fabric only brushes my hips as I walk, and I truly feel beautiful in this dress. I don't think Abri is getting this back.

Then I put the shoes on…

Yeah, this outfit is mine now.

I snap a mirror selfie and send it to Abri, and she immediately replies with about ten fire emojis, boosting my confidence even more.

I swipe on a deep red lipstick that adds another layer of confidence as the finishing touch, and check my phone. I have just enough time to do one more thing before meeting Santino.

Only putting the necessities in my purse, I ride the elevator down to the basement and am relieved to see it's empty. I head straight for the knife-throwing room and to the cabinet in the back. There's scarily a lot of choices in here.

Hanging on the side of one of the walls is a thigh holster that can hold up to three knives, and I take it out, strapping it around my upper right thigh. I look through my knife choices and pick out three folding knives that will lay flat enough against my leg so that when I let my dress fall back into place, you can't even tell I have anything on under here.

I practice walking around the room to make sure the holster is secure. I don't know what I'm walking into with this fight night shit, but I want to be prepared. I know I can't hold my own against a room of grown men trained to kill, but I sure as hell can even the playing field a little.

Taking a deep breath, I close my eyes and let my mask slip into place. I haven't had to wear it around Dante, so it takes a little more effort than usual, but when I let the false me take over, it doesn't seem so false anymore.

Even the fake me is a part of me.

I don't need to fake the confidence and don't-give-a-fuck attitude anymore. It is me. I am her.

It's just about channeling my Carfano blood and sending the softer parts of me to the back. I used to think I was burying who I was to be someone else for my family in order to please them, but now I realize it's a power. I feel like I'm finally coming into my own and am only just tapping into everything I'm capable of.

I spot myself in the wall of mirrors in the gym as I'm walking back to the elevators and love the woman looking back at me. She looks like she can take on the world and come out on top without even breaking a nail.

Taking the elevator up to the garage, I walk through it and punch in my code to open a side door that leads to the street. Santino is already there waiting, leaning against his car with his arms crossed over his chest. The moment he sees me, he straightens, his eyes raking down my body.

CHAPTER 23

Katarina

Santino opens the back door of his car for me without a word and I get in, careful with my dress.

"Where are we going?" I ask him when he gets in on the other side.

His driver pulls away from the curb and Santino clears his throat. "The basement of a warehouse in Hell's Kitchen. I know you think you can handle yourself in there, but I'm going to have to ask you to stay by my side when we arrive."

"That's fine," I agree, and his eyes dart down to mine. "What? I don't want my family to see me right away. So as long as you can assure me I won't be seen by them or manhandled by some assholes, then you can be sure I won't let Dante or Leo kill you."

"You didn't seem this ruthless when we first met."

"I know." I smirk, and he shakes his head in disbelief.

"If you didn't already tell me you were with The Executioner himself, then I'd insist we get married right now."

I can't help but laugh. "So, you like your women ruthless and manipulative?"

"Don't forget gorgeous beyond belief."

"Of course. Because then her personality can be overlooked."

"No. I like the whole package. Crazy and beautiful."

"You're an odd one, Santino."

He flashes me a wide grin. "I know. Now, Dom"—he nods to the man who's been silent in the passenger's seat—"will be with us, and I want to make sure you're always between us. I don't want you getting lost in there. The crowd can get pretty wild once the fights start."

"How many are there?"

"Tonight, there are six, and each one has three, five-minute rounds. I asked my contact for the order, and the Carfano/Aleksanyan fight is last. I'm assuming Leo has a plan in the works because my contact still thinks someone else is representing your family."

"He does."

"Good. Hovan threatened and manipulated my father, and got you shot."

"And this will bring us one step closer to the man he hired to do that."

"I'm sorry about that, you know. My father..." He

shakes his head regretfully. "I didn't know that entire lunch was a set up. He made me look like an accomplice and like a fucking idiot when Leo had us come back to talk."

I don't exactly know how to respond, because I sure as hell am not going to console him. He should've known. He's known his father his whole life and was in line to take over some day. I know from watching Leo and my father my entire childhood that that means you're with them all the time, learning and watching. Santino had to know something, or at least have had an idea.

The car pulls up to a building and Santino removes a gun from his hip and hands it to his driver. "You don't have any weapons, right?" he asks. "They're strictly forbidden and they're going to pat you down."

"No," I lie. "I couldn't fit my gun in this purse," I tease, and he grins, getting out of the car with Dom, who looks around and then opens my door.

There are two men on either side of the door we approach, who both step in front of it to stop us from entering. Santino pulls out a card of some kind from his pocket and shows it to the guards. They nod and hand it back, then proceed to pat down Dom and Santino. They check my purse next, but I stop them before they can pat me down.

"Does it look like I'm hiding a weapon on me?" I ask, and they immediately take the opportunity to check me out.

"It's policy," one of them grunts out, and I push my hair over my shoulder.

"You're not touching me," I sneer. I can tell Santino is about to step in and defend me, but I beat him to it, raising my chin. "I'm Katarina Carfano. I can have Leo and Luca come out here and explain to you how you're not touching me. Or better yet, my fiancé would love it if I told him you put your hands on me." I can see they're about to challenge me, until I utter his name. "Dante Salerno. I'm sure he'd enjoy showing you how he got the name The Executioner."

Recognition and fear immediately flash through the eyes of these grown men, and then they look at each other. "Understood, Miss Carfano," one of them says, and they step aside. Dom opens the door and we pass through, a mix of relief and power coursing through me.

"Impressive," Santino praises when the heavy metal door closes behind us. I flash him a quick grin and then make my face go emotionless again, keeping my shoulders pulled back while we walk through the abandoned warehouse to the industrial elevator.

We ride it down a level and I hear the yelling before Dom can even reach down and pull the metal door of the elevator up. I drop my hand to my thigh, feeling the outline of the knives to remind myself that no matter what I'm walking into, I can protect myself.

But when the door is lifted, I'm momentarily stunned, assaulted by the sheer volume and energy of this place. Sections are roped off in triangles, like pizza slices radiating out from the cage in the middle of the room.

Santino knows better than to touch me, but he leans in close to tell me, "Stay between us. We're going to walk the perimeter until we get to my family's section."

"Okay," I reply, but I know he can't hear me, so I nod my acknowledgment and he takes his place behind me.

There's a match happening right now, which means everyone in the room is too preoccupied to notice me sandwiched between these two men. No one would recognize me anyhow. Only those my father would bring over for dinner or those in attendance of the charity events I sometimes attended with the family would know who I am.

It's wild in here. The sound of fists hitting flesh and the chanting and yelling of the crowd has me wondering what will happen when Dante comes out.

I follow Dom into a section that has their own guard at the entrance, and Santino and him exchange words before he comes to stand beside me in the back. "They're on the fourth fight," he tells me. "You can have a seat back here if you'd like. Your family's section is directly across from us. They can't see you with the cage between us, but if you move closer, they might."

"Thanks. I'll hang back here."

Nodding, he takes a seat beside me, and because the cage is on a raised platform, I can still see everything from back here. I don't need to actually get blood on me to enjoy the primal, brutal violence happening before my eyes.

When I first learned what MMA was, I was confused as to why anyone would subject themselves to that, and wondered who would enjoy watching two people beat the shit out of each other. But after two minutes of watching it live, I get it. I can't look away. I want to, but I can't.

"Who's up there?"

"The guy in the blue shorts is from the Capriglione family, and the one in the green is from the O'Leary family."

"Italian versus Irish."

"The Irish are scrappy. I never underestimate whoever they enter."

And he's right. It looks like he's losing, but in the third round, he gets a burst of energy and beats his opponent's ass until he's lying motionless on the mat.

"That was more satisfying to watch than I thought it'd be," I admit, and Santino laughs.

"It always is."

The next fight starts ten minutes later, and the Albanian wins over the man representing the Yakuza. That one was fun to watch, too. They had two very different fighting styles and approaches to how they attacked one another.

Dante is next, and waiting those ten minutes for him to come out feels like an hour.

I'm jittery, so I cross my legs to keep from jiggling my knee like a nervous schoolgirl, but then quickly uncross them because my dress rides up and I don't need anyone spotting the holster I have on under here.

I don't think I've ever suppressed my emotions as much as I am in this moment. It all tightens into a ball that sits like a knotted string of Christmas lights in my stomach, with lights popping on and off and short circuiting, sending shockwaves through me that I act like aren't happening.

"Is Hovan here? Do you see him?" I ask Santino, and he looks around.

"He's at our three o'clock," he tells me, and I casually turn my head to the right. "The man who just stood up in the pinstripe suit with a white shirt and sunglasses hanging from the opening."

I find him, seeing a smug look on his face as he turns

towards where Leo and Luca are sitting. I can't see my brothers from here, but I know they must be fuming, and it's taking everything in them to not do something with him so close.

The announcer comes to the center of the cage and the crowd lowers in volume.

"We saved the best for last, everyone. Representing the Armenians tonight, we have a new face. Brought over all the way from Armenia…Abaven Margosian!" The room erupts as he emerges from the doorway on one side of the room and takes his time walking to the cage.

Holy hell, who is this guy?

He's massive. Like, 6'7" massive, with muscles for days. It looks like he could snap a tree in half if given the chance.

But I know Dante is good. He's been training his entire life for this. The big and powerful always have a weak spot, and I know Dante's already done his research and knows exactly what his is.

"And for the Carfano family, we have a little change in the program," the announcer says, and a wave of mumbling rolls through the crowd. "A little treat, if you will," he teases.

I look over to Hovan and see the smugness wiped from his face, replaced by anger. He didn't think we'd find out about his plan…

"He hasn't been in this cage in quite some time," the announcer continues, "but I know you all know who he is by reputation alone, and that this will be one hell of a match." All eyes turn towards the same doorway that monster of a man just emerged from. "Welcome back to the cage…THE EXEUCUTIONER!" he bellows, and the room erupts.

Holy shit, I wasn't expecting that.

Standing, I watch Dante walk the same path through the crowd as Abaven, his face blank.

I'm seeing him how everyone else does and he's sexy as hell. This man — *my man* — is known by everyone here as someone who wins. As someone who is superior. It's the only place he steps out of the shadows and receives praise and recognition. He's ignoring everyone, though. His gaze is straight ahead on the cage and on his opponent.

He's in the zone.

I remain where I am, not wanting him or my brothers to see me. I don't want to be a distraction or cause a scene before Dante can take this hulk out and show Hovan that my family can't be played.

Inside the cage, Dante and Abaven circle each other, sizing one another up. Dante is calm and composed while Abaven is jumping from foot to foot and stretching his neck out. He's making a show of it, attempting to psych-out a man who can't be psyched-out. That's his first mistake.

His second mistake is making the first move. He's entering Dante's space, and Dante quickly blocks the first strike and gets in two quick jabs of his own. I know nothing about the rules or the moves and combinations, but watching Dante's body move is mesmerizing.

Five minutes feels like a lifetime as they each get their hits and kicks in, until Dante is able to grab Abaven around his shoulders and knee him in the ribs three times just as the horn blares to signify the end of the first round.

I breathe a sigh of relief. "Who's winning?" I ask Santino.

"It's pretty even."

Sighing, I play with the ends of my hair, needing this to move along. Dante shoots water into his mouth and wipes blood from his brow. I can already see one of his eyes starting to swell from here and the cuts he got a few days ago have reopened and are bleeding down his face.

The second round is worse. Abaven is able to land a few kicks to Dante's ribs, but Dante is able to rush him and throw him down to the mat, right on his spine. Abaven rolls away and sweeps his leg out to bring Dante down with him and pins him with his body.

Abaven lands blow after blow until Dante manages to wrap a leg around him and roll him over to get the upper hand. He has Abaven in a hold he can't escape and the beast in Dante takes over. He hits him until his face is a bloody mess, sending castoff onto his bare chest and arms.

The round ends and Dante stands. His chest heaves with labored breaths, his nostrils are flared, and his dark eyes are focused on the man at his feet.

I wish I knew what he was thinking.

I'm glad Santino doesn't try to talk to me, because I have no words.

The horn blares for the third round, and my anxiety has my nerves strung out. I need a drink. I need five drinks. But I have to keep my head straight in a room like this.

Abaven pounds on the cage and looks out to Hovan in the crowd, who gives him a nod with a manic little grin that has my palms sweating and my heart racing.

Something's going to happen.

They've planned something.

Circling each other, Abaven moves into Dante's space, but Dante blocks his punch and lands a string of his own. Abaven grabs Dante and knees him in his ribs until Dante manages to block him and takes a few steps back.

Abaven's bloody and bruised face twists with a gnarly grin and he charges at Dante, but he twists out of the way and lands a punch to Abaven's lower back, right over his kidneys. Grunting, Abaven shoves his hand in the pocket of his shorts and comes back out with a switchblade.

I jump to my feet.

No!

Dante doesn't have a visual of Abaven's hand yet, so when he makes his move, Dante is caught completely off guard.

His hand comes up quick, slashing at Dante's chest and torso like he's having an invisible sword fight, slicing Dante open.

He doesn't grunt. He doesn't yell. He doesn't make a sound of discomfort or pain at all.

Abaven takes a step back and laughs manically at his work while the crowd roars with a mix of cheers and outbursts of anger. There's supposed to be no weapons allowed!

I can see Leo and Luca across the way now, shouting at the announcer to do something, but he raises his hands in defeat. He's not going in the cage with that maniac.

Leo rubs his jaw and talks low with Luca while Dante is being sliced alive in a fight he made him enter.

Anger boils my blood, catching fire to where every beat of my heart feels like a burst of oxygen to an open flame, spreading the fire to every corner of my body.

Dante looks down at his chest and then up at Abaven, unfazed. He stalks towards his opponent, blocking the first two strikes Abaven tries to make, but then he can't block the next, and Abaven stabs him in the side.

He goes down.

"Dante!" I scream, rushing to the front of the Antonucci's section, gaining the stares of everyone around me. But all I see is Dante lying on the mat, his entire torso covered in blood that keeps flowing out of him.

"Get up and fight!" I yell, and his head slowly turns to the side, his eyes finding mine. "You promised me you wouldn't die!"

I'm so fucking angry.

If he doesn't get up and kill this piece of shit, I'll do it for him.

"Dante!" I scream his name again, and it's as if he snaps back to reality, realizing where he is. He rolls away from Abaven and stands, not even wincing at the fact that he was just stabbed.

His eyes flit to mine again and his emotionless face thunders as he goes after Abaven. He blocks Abaven's attempt to stab him again with his forearm and then punches him in the throat.

Abaven's face turns red as he tries to gasp for air. He starts to swipe the knife in the space between them to keep Dante away, but Dante grabs his wrist mid-air and bends it inward, forcing him to stab himself in the gut.

A gargled sound comes from his crushed throat, but Dante isn't done yet. He twists the blade inside of him and punches him in the throat again, making Abaven completely under Dante's control.

Taking the knife from his loosened grip, Dante stabs him twice more and he stumbles backwards. Dante goes after him and finishes him off with a slash of the knife across his throat.

Abaven falls to his knees, his hands wrapped around his throat to try to hold the blood in, but it's no use. His eyes widen and he opens and closes his mouth, trying and failing to speak.

Dante turns to look at Hovan and I follow his gaze. That asshole moved up to the cage like I did, but now he spins on his heel and walks back in a rush, trying to make a quick exit. I see Leo and Luca yelling at their men to get him, but there's a crowd between them and I'm closer.

"Kat, no." Santino grabs my arm to try to stop me, but I use the new defensive move I learned and easily break free.

Seeing Dante almost die in front of me and watching my brothers do absolutely nothing to try to help him, has my already boiling blood turning into steam and evaporating. I'm done. I'm so fucking done.

My source of humanity and life leaves me and what takes its place is pure hatred.

Everyone in here is too engrossed with what just happened in the cage to know the war that was just activated. I walk through the Antonucci's section, already knowing my next move.

I fluff my hair out and wait for Hovan as he moves through everyone. When he's close, I fake a stumble in my heels and land against him, pushing us up against the cement wall.

"Oh, my God," I gush, feigning stupidity. "I'm so sorry! I guess these heels were a bad idea." Laughing, I smile up at him.

Righting me on my feet, he looks me up and down, with no recognition in his eyes as to who I am. He must've not seen me yelling at Dante. "Those shoes were the perfect choice," he says with a thick accent, and the men around him turn to face the other direction to give us some privacy.

Smiling seductively, I squeeze his arm. "Thank you."

"Are you here with anyone? I can't imagine a woman as beautiful as you is alone in a room like this."

"Well, aren't you sweet?" I flirt, and he flashes me a wicked grin.

"I am anything but sweet, honey."

I smile and keep eye contact with him as I reach under my dress and slip one of my knives out. Flicking it open, I drop my smile and all pretenses. "Oh, I know," I say, and shove my blade into his thigh. "I'm Katarina Carfano."

He lets out a low groan of pain, but his men don't hear him over the noise of the crowd. Hovan gets this wild look in his eyes and grabs me by the throat. I pull the knife out and shove it back in the same thigh, causing his grip to loosen, which is when I pull the knife free and press it to his throat.

He laughs.

He fucking laughs and holds his hands up.

"A beautiful woman holds a knife to my throat and just like that, I'm in love. You want to play, honey?"

"I don't have time to play. You tried to kill me and my family, and tonight you had your fighter try to kill my fiancé."

"Your fiancé?" he scoffs, and I press the blade into his flesh, blood starting to trickle down his neck.

"Yes," I hiss. "You decided to fuck with the wrong family."

"You might want to hear what I know about your family before you try to kill me."

"Why?"

"Because I know what really happened to your father and uncle."

"They were shot and killed. Everyone knows that."

"But I know that the hit came from someone inside your family."

I press the edge of the blade into him even more, showing Hovan I'm not to be fucked with. "You're lying."

"Why would I lie? I have nothing to gain from it."

"I've got it from here, Kat," I hear Leo say behind me, but I'm too lost in the game Hovan is trying to play to give up just yet.

"I've got it," I growl, my voice unrecognizable to my own ears.

"You did good, Kat. I need him alive for a little while longer, though."

I know he's right. We need him to find the sniper.

"Kat, Dante needs you. I've got this."

At the mention of Dante, I immediately step back, and Hovan laughs. "Your sister is a little crazy, Leo. I think I'm in love."

"Shut the fuck up," Leo snarls as his men take Hovan by the arms and lead him out of the building.

"You might need this," I say, slapping the bloody knife

to Leo's chest. "I have two more."

He takes the knife, but I see it in his eyes that he's pissed at me. "We're going to talk later about why the fuck you're here, and *how* you got here."

"It's pretty simple. I blackmailed Santino into taking me," I tell him smugly. "And I came for Dante." Looking back at the cage, I only see Abaven lying dead and my heart drops. "Where is he? Where did he go?"

Santino approaches us, holding my purse that I hadn't even realized I left stranded.

"Where is he," I repeat, sounding panicked.

"They took him out of here."

"Who?"

"Luca and a couple guys. He was trying to get to you but was losing too much blood."

"Let's go. We need to go right now," I say to Santino, but Leo interrupts.

"You're coming with me."

"I'm not riding in the car with that piece of shit or sandwiched between your soldiers."

Leo's face reddens with how hard he's holding back from arguing with me, and instead addresses Santino. "You get her out of here and home safely or—"

"Or you'll kill me," he finishes for Leo. "I'm pretty accustomed to the threat now."

Dom makes a path for us out of there and we find his driver waiting at the end of the block.

I'm glad he doesn't try to say anything to me on the ride back, and I only manage to mutter a quick 'thank you' before I fling the car door open and rush into my family's building.

My heels slip on the marble flooring in the lobby, but it only slows me down a fraction before I'm pounding my finger into the elevator's button, begging it to arrive faster. I do the same when I'm inside the car, pressing the button for the medical suite repeatedly until the doors close.

He can't die.

He can't leave me.

The elevator finally opens again and I run out, my feet blindly carrying me down the hall until I'm stopped by a pair of arms that wrap around me.

"You can't go in there," Luca tells me, and I fight against him.

"I need to!" I look through the window of the door behind him and see Dante laid out on the operating table, covered in blood, as a nurse places a mask over his mouth and nose and the doctor barks out orders to his team.

Seeing him like that has my legs threatening to give out, but Luca tightens his arms around me and walks me to the nearest chair.

"He's going to be okay, Kat. Doc will do everything in is power to save him."

"He better. Or he's the first to die."

Luca lets out a dark little chuckle, pulling me in for a hug just as the first tear falls down my cheek.

CHAPTER 24
Dante

"Katarina? Where is she?" I ask as I'm being helped out of the cage. The room is blurry and I can't feel my legs, but I manage to stay upright.

"She's fucking up Hovan," Luca tells me, wrapping one of my arms around his shoulder.

"What?" Straightening, I try to look around for her, but all I see a blur of black and white.

Fuck, that fucker caught me off guard. No one catches me off guard.

"Don't worry, Leo's got her. Just walk. We have to get the hell out of here."

"I told her not to come. How did she get here?"

"Not with us," he says, grunting as I lean on him. "Stop asking questions and walk. She'll be fine. But you won't be if I don't get you out of here."

We make our way back to the makeshift locker room area and out a side door where an SUV is already waiting with Jimmy behind the wheel. Luca opens the back door and helps me up inside. I lay out across the seat and he goes to the trunk, tossing a mix of towels and t-shirts over the seat to me.

"Put pressure on your wounds. I don't want Kat coming after me if you die on the way. I saw how she yelled at you to get your ass up and finish the fight, and I just saw her put a knife to Hovan's throat."

The corners of my mouth turn up. "My girl is good."

Luca calls the doctor and tells him to meet us at the suite with his on-call surgical team, and then he distracts me by asking, "You teach her that?"

"The yelling at me or the knife?"

"Both, I guess. She's never yelled at anyone."

"She already knows how to shoot a gun, so I taught her a few knife moves."

"She can shoot?"

"You don't know her as well as you think." My voice is gravelly. I'm fighting the pull to close my eyes and save my energy, but I know I need to keep talking. I need to stay alert.

"And you do?"

"Yes." I cough. "I've watched her for years. I know almost everything about her."

"You've been watching my sister?"

"Yes." I don't need to explain myself to anyone, and I

don't have the energy to do it either. He's acting like I'm the asshole, when he's the one who kidnapped Angela. She's a fucking Cicariello. Her father and the rest of her family were pieces of shit, though, so she was saved in my opinion, but Luca doesn't really have a moral high ground to stand on here.

"If you do anything to hurt her, I'll kill you. Whatever you may think or feel on the matter of how you came into our family, I've always considered you like another brother. But that won't save you if you do anything to hurt Kat. Understand?"

"Understood."

I press the t-shirts against my side and chest harder and grunt. *Fuck.*

"We're here, man," Luca says as Jimmy pulls into the garage and right up to the elevators. I manage to sit up and get out myself, but Luca is right there to wrap my arm around his shoulder for support.

"Let me help you," he says angrily. "I don't even know how you're standing right now with how much blood you've lost."

"I've had worse," I grumble, and Luca shakes his head. Although, I think he might be right about the blood loss, because by the time we make it up to the medical suite, I need the doctor's help to make it to the nearest room and up on the table.

People swarm around me and my eyes grow heavy. "Katarina," I mumble, but I don't know if anyone hears me. "Katarina."

"She'll be here when you wake up," someone tells me as

a mask is put over my nose and mouth, and I keep saying her name until the darkness pulls me under.

CHAPTER 25

Dante

I blink my eyes open and am met with a stark white ceiling. I try to move, but my body hasn't woken yet from the anesthesia or whatever the fuck they gave me.

It takes a few minutes, but I fight through the thick cloud weighing me down and I feel around for the button that raises the bed so I can sit up.

"What are you doing?" Katarina's angry angelic voice cuts through the rest of my haze and she appears above me. She places her hand over mine to stop me from finding the button. "You can't sit up yet."

"I'm fine, babygirl."

Her eyes fill with tears and she cups my cheek, leaning

down to press her forehead to mine. "I thought I was going to lose you," she whispers, her tears falling onto my face.

"I told you I'd come home to you. I don't break my promises."

Bending down, she kisses me softly at first, until it's too delicate and she deepens it, giving me all of her worry and relief. Or is it my relief I'm feeling that I get to kiss her again at all?

Sitting down in the chair she's pulled up beside my bed, Katarina takes my hand in hers. "Why were you there?" I ask her. "I told you I didn't want you there."

"I had every right to be there," she fires back, then rubs her forehead, softening. "You needed me, Dante."

"I did," I agree, and she squeezes my hand. "You weren't with your brothers, though." I remember looking to the side and seeing her, but that it wasn't the side of the cage where Leo and Luca were.

"No, I wasn't."

"Then who were you with? How did you get there?"

"Is this what you want to talk about when you've just woken up?"

"Yes," I tell her, and see the worry on her face.

"I called Santino and blackmailed him into picking me up and taking me." I stare at her, shocked. "I told him if he did, then it would be a good gesture of trust to Leo after everything with his father. I also said I would make sure you and Leo wouldn't kill him."

"And what did you tell him would happen if he said no?"

"I told him I was marrying you and not him, and that I'd

tell you that he was no longer needed in any business deals with the family."

"You told him I'd kill him?" I ask in disbelief, and she nods with a sly little grin.

"I did. Is that a problem?"

"Not at all, babygirl. I've already thought about killing him hundreds of times since your father told me he was the one you were to marry."

She freezes. "What?"

Fuck, the drugs must still be clouding my brain. "Nothing," I say quickly, but she's not buying it.

"My father told you when he was still alive that he wanted me with Santino? He told me I was going to be married off to the man of his choosing after I turned eighteen, but he never told me who. Did everyone know? Then why now? Why was Leo following through with it when I'm twenty-fucking-two?"

Standing abruptly, she paces the small room, and I notice for the first time that she's wearing a sexy little dress. "How long have you been here? You're still in a dress. Did you wear that to the fight?"

"Are you seriously ignoring everything I just asked you? I've been here all night and morning, waiting for you to wake up."

"Come sit back down. I'll answer your questions if you come back."

Her anger fades just the slightest, and she takes her place by my side again.

"I already told you that Michael told me to stay away from you. What I left out was that he sat me in his office, took his gun out, and told me he would kill me himself if he ever saw me looking at you the way I was again. And I wanted to do more than just look at you, babygirl, but he brought me into his home and trained me to be a protector for his family, not to take his daughter."

"He was an asshole, Dante. He made me miserable my entire life. Controlling me, putting me down, and raising me to be someone he could use in a business deal rather than a strong woman who could stand on her own two feet."

"You didn't need him to teach you that last one. You already are a strong woman who stands on her own two feet. That's not something you can even teach. That comes from within, Katarina."

She looks at her hands. "I've never said this out loud before, but I'm glad he's gone." Her confession hits me square in the chest. "He would yell at and berate my mom, and sometimes handle her forcefully. She hid it well. You can hide a lot in a house that size with walls thick enough to contain its secrets. But I saw her bruises when she would be cooking and she pushed her sleeves up to wash her hands or something. She'd forget and then see me staring and push them back down. I knew she was ashamed to have me see, but she never said anything. She never confided in me. She just pretended nothing was going on."

"He put his hands on her?" Anger surges through me with flashbacks of my own father getting drunk and shoving my mom around. My hand is shaking with the urge to bring Michael back from the grave so I can kill him myself. "Did he hurt you?"

"Not physically. No." My anger only lessens marginally

at her confirmation. "No one else knew about him and my mom. My brothers never saw or heard anything when they lived at home. Hell, I didn't even notice until I was a teenager. Alec was in Atlantic City with uncle Sal, and Leo and Luca were too busy here in the city doing whatever it is they were doing to know or notice. It was just my mom and I in that house with him."

"And I wasn't there."

"No, you weren't."

"I should've seen the signs. If I saw something, babygirl, I would've..." I shake my head.

She gives me a soft smile. "It's okay, Dante. It's in the past. You want to hear something odd, though?" she asks, changing subjects. "Hovan told me something before Leo took him away."

"What?"

"He said he knows something about my father and uncle's deaths. He said the hit came from within the family, but everyone knows the Cicariellos did it."

What the fuck?

"He's just trying to prolong his life, Katarina. He thinks you'll be the most sympathetic."

"Really? Because he said it to me when I had a knife to his throat after I already stabbed him in the leg. Twice."

"You did what?" I ask, thinking maybe I'm hearing things. She bites her bottom lip, fighting a grin, and I reach up to pull her lip free. "Were you a little ruthless for me?"

"I was."

"How did you get a knife in there?"

Turning her head, she kisses my palm and stands, lifting

the dress she still has on from last night. I lick my lips, needing a taste of her heaven to make this dull pain go away, but my eyes stray from her covered pussy to see a holster strapped to her upper thigh with two knives folded and in their slots.

"I told them who I was at the door and that if they touched me, then they'd have to deal with you."

Groaning, I slide my hand up her thigh. "You don't know how fucking sexy I find that, babygirl. You used my name twice in one night as a threat to get what you wanted."

"You don't mind?" she teases, and I grip the back of her thigh and pull her forward. Her hands come down to the bed beside me to brace herself.

"Mind? If I could fuck you right now, I would. I only wish I heard you use me as a threat."

Smiling seductively, Katarina kisses her way up the scar on my face. "I'm sure one day you will," she whispers in my ear. "But since you can't fuck me, how about I show you how happy I am that you're alive?"

My cock hardens at her words and she steps away to lock the door and roll a divider curtain over to block the window on it.

"I don't like that you had that asshole take you to the fight dressed like that. You look too good, babygirl."

"I didn't realize someone could look too good."

"That's you all the time."

Her cheeks turn a pretty shade of pink as she pulls the sheet from my body. She looks at the five new bandages covering my chest and torso, and her fingertips skim over me, around the bandages and down to the waistband of my boxers. I'll have to thank the good doctor for cleaning me up for this exact moment.

My muscles flex under her light touch.

"More scars," I say passively, not really sure why.

"They tell your life's story," she says softly. "Each one shows you're a survivor, and I love them like I love you."

"Say it again."

"Which part?"

"You know which part."

Slipping her hand inside my boxers, she pulls my dick out, sliding her hand up and down my length. "I love you," she repeats, and I groan, which has her smiling like she's caught her prey in her trap. And she has. Being her prey to catch and consume is the greatest fucking gift in the world.

Katarina climbs up on the bed and straddles my thighs, her dress riding up to her hips in the process to show me that sexy holster and her black satin-covered pussy.

"I'm not hurting you, am I?"

"No," I choke out. "Never."

"Good."

Gripping the base of my cock with one hand, Katarina dips down and takes the head of my cock in her hot little mouth. I know she's never done this before, so I let her get used to it. I let her explore.

She takes as much of me as she can and then comes back up for air. Swirling her tongue around my swollen head, she moans and bobs back down my length, this time using her hand to meet her when she can't take any more.

"Fuck," I grunt. "That's it, babygirl. Take me how you want me. Show me you love having my cock in your mouth."

I look down to see her lips stretched wide around me, and the sight is sexier than I imagined.

That dress.

Her straddling me.

Her moaning while choking on my dick.

Her hair a curtain of brown and gold silk spun together in a wave that brushes my hips and thighs in a seductive caress.

It doesn't take long for me to feel the tightening of my balls and the lightning coursing down my spine.

I can feel her hips rocking, but I know she's not getting what she needs. I sit up just enough to move her so she's straddling one of my thighs. "Ride my leg, babygirl. Suck me off and rub your pussy all over my leg to show me how much you love having my cock in your mouth."

Katarina moans around me, the vibrations rippling through me in waves as she rubs her hot pussy on my thigh.

"Suck me harder," I grunt out, and her hand at the base of my cock squeezes me like she's trying to cut off my circulation while her hot mouth sucks me like a fucking vacuum.

"Fuuuucckkk," I groan, every new cut on my body screaming from the pressure inside of me.

The hand she has braced on my thigh curls inward, her nails pressing into me. I hope she breaks skin. I want her scars on me, too.

Grinding down harder on my thigh, Katarina finds a rhythm that's driving me crazy. "Get there with me," I tell her, and she moves against me quicker.

Katarina swirls her tongue around my head and sucks on

it so fucking hard that she sucks my fucking orgasm right out of me.

Mine and Katarina's groans fill the room, and she swallows every drop of come I shoot down her throat like the good fucking girl she is.

She releases me with wet pop, her eyes lifting to mine, showing me everything. I won't ever tire of being able to see her like this — open and vulnerable.

"Come lay with me," I rasp, and she crawls over me to my side without the stab wound. Her wet silk panties drag over my thighs and I suck in a sharp breath.

"Did I hurt you?"

"Far from it, babygirl." Her concern for me makes me love her even more, and I wrap my arm around her, tucking her against me.

Getting comfortable, she hooks one of her long, sexy legs over mine and drapes her arm over my lower stomach where there aren't any bandages.

"I've come in your pussy and your mouth. Now I have to come in your ass and every part of you will be mine."

She chokes on a little moan. "All of me is already yours."

"In every aspect but one."

"Then we should change that," she whispers, kissing my chest.

I go instantly hard, wanting my cock to be strangled by her tight little ass. "You're not ready yet, babygirl."

"Then you'll have to get me ready," she mumbles. "But just so we're clear, if you ever try to tell me I can't go somewhere again like you did yesterday, then you'll never fully have me. Got it?"

On cue, my new wounds throb. "I got it. But just so you know, I want to fight you on it but I'm not going to because I want to see you use a knife on someone for myself."

I feel her smile against me. "That can be arranged."

"My ruthless little hellion."

Her smile against me grows and she licks the side of my chest, sinking her teeth into me. "Always remember that."

CHAPTER 26
Katarina

I stir awake when I hear Dante groaning in pain, and I lift my head to find his eyes still closed. I know he has too much pride to admit that he's in any amount of pain, but by the sound he just made, I know whatever the doctor gave him is wearing off and he's feeling every inch of those slashes on his body.

I look around for the pain medication button I saw the doctor use before he left, hoping I don't wake him before I do. Reaching back, I dig my hand in the crease between the bed and the short side rail, and silently cheer when I come up with the cord.

Feeling for the end of it, I look up at the monitor he's

still hooked up to on the other side of the bed and press the button a couple times until his breathing and the spikes in his heart rate even out to a steady rhythm.

I wait a few more minutes and then slip from the bed. Covering him with the sheet, I move the room divider as quietly as I can and look back at Dante sleeping soundly before leaving.

I stayed by his side all night and morning while he was in surgery and recovering, and then laid with him all afternoon and evening. I just need to take a shower, change my clothes, and eat something before my stomach eats itself.

I never gave Leo a list of groceries though, so I make myself toast, eggs, and a fresh cup of coffee, and I feel revitalized despite my lack of sleep.

My mind won't shut off or stop replaying everything that happened. Seeing Dante like that...covered in blood...

It wasn't easy, and I snapped, needing to make that bastard who put him in that position pay. I've never hurt anyone before last night, and I'm oddly only slightly alarmed by the fact that I didn't hesitate to inflict pain like I did.

One thing my mind can't seem to leave alone is what Hovan said to me. He already knew his fate with my family if he was caught before he could kill us, so why say something like that?

I want to be with Dante so he's not alone when he wakes up again, but I can't sit there for hours while he sleeps with all of these unanswered questions swirling around in my head. Something in me is telling me I need to go and get the answers myself.

I don't owe my father anything, but if there's someone in

my family who put the hit on him and my uncle, then I can't help thinking it might've been Leo or Alec, or both.

Leo and Alec took their places.

Uncle Sal taught Alec everything he knows, and he was more than ready to take over running our family's casino in Atlantic City after it all happened. In fact, everyone was. The older generation faded to the background and my brothers and cousins stepped into their new roles under the leadership of Leo.

I have to know if it was them or someone else. Maybe someone who thought taking out my father would get them one step closer to the role they want — the boss. That would mean Leo is now vulnerable too.

Now that my stomach isn't screaming at me, I take a shower and dress in black leggings and an oversized black sweatshirt. I don't want anyone down there when I go, so I wait a couple hours until it's past midnight. On the ride down to the basement, I try to come up with an excuse to give anyone who might still be down there, but luckily I don't have to worry about it. The place is empty and dead silent, and half the lights are off.

I walk through the gym area and stop at the start of the hall where it's just cement walls and doors.

Am I really going to do this?

I don't know what or who else I'm going to find down here besides Hovan, and as I approach the first door, I breathe out a sigh of relief that I'm not going to have to find out since it's Hovan I see through the small window in the door. He's sitting on a flat mattress on the floor with his back against the wall and his eyes closed. His leg is shackled with a cuff at his ankle and a long chain that's anchored to the wall, so I know when I open the door, he can't overpower me and escape.

I pull on the handle, but it's locked. Shit, I need a key. It has to be around here somewhere.

I search the conference room, my eyes sweeping everywhere until they land on a silver box on the wall like you'd find at a valet stand. Inside, there are keys to everything down here, and I grab the one labeled 'cell 1'.

I start to leave, but then realize I can't go in there unarmed, even if he is shackled. Turning down the hall Dante took me down, I pass the shooting range and stand in front of the artillery doors, racking my brain to remember the code I saw Dante punch in.

Think, think, think.

I close my eyes and picture him pressing the buttons.

I think it was…

I punch in six numbers and the green light flashes. Yes!

Once inside, I look around and decide on a couple pocket knives that I shove in the side pockets of my leggings, and then load up a nine-millimeter handgun and put that in the front pocket of my sweatshirt.

Closing the door behind me, I make sure it's locked again and I take a moment to pace the hallway near Hovan's cell to gain the composure I need to do this. I want to and have to, but that doesn't mean I'm any less nervous about being alone down here with a psychopath who wants me and my family dead.

I let out a rush of air. "Okay," I whisper to myself, and unlock the door. The sound is deafeningly loud in the silence and Hovan's eyes pop open and snap to mine, his manic grin instant.

I open the heavy metal door, but I don't go in. Not yet.

"Hello, beautiful Katarina. Are you here to hurt me a little more?" The unhinged look in his eyes is telling me he wouldn't mind in the least if I came in there and inflicted a little more pain on him.

"And if I told you I was?"

"Then I'd die a happy man."

"I'm here because of what you said to me."

"I say so many things."

"You said the hit on my father and uncle came from within the family. Who was it?"

"I never said I knew."

"If you didn't know, you wouldn't have used it as a ploy to try to get me to prolong your life."

"Is that what I was doing?"

"Stop playing games," I demand, and he laughs.

"I'm a dead man either way, honey. Why not have a little fun before I go out?"

"Because you can either go out at the hands of my brothers and Dante, or me. If you tell me what I want to know, I'll let you choose how you die."

That sparks interest in his eyes. "What an intriguing offer."

"It is an intriguing offer, and one you won't get from anyone else. You're going to tell me how to find the sniper you hired that shot me, and then you're going to tell me who put the hit on my father and uncle."

"I never instructed the sniper to shoot you. He told me

you were right there in the window and seemed like a good place to start. You know, he really is a sick bastard. And that's saying something coming from me."

"How do we find him?"

"I contacted him through an ally back home who had used him for a few jobs. He never takes jobs here in the US because he doesn't like to leave a trace of entering a country with a passport. But my offer was too generous to pass up."

"And where is he now?"

"I don't know." He shrugs.

"How did you contact him when he got here?"

"Ah, clever and beautiful. You have to know the right questions to ask when you're interrogating someone."

"Thanks for the tip," I deadpan. "Do you have a phone number for him or know where he's staying?"

"I do, but he's smart. He'll know it's not me. There's a no-contact rule until after the job is done."

"So he's still hunting us?"

"He is." Hovan grins.

"You do realize that if we're all killed, then no one will be letting you out and you'll just rot and die in here from any number of things. Starvation, dehydration, some kind of infection…you name it."

"True." He nods, looking me up and down. "Did you come in here unarmed?"

"No."

His eyes light up. "What did you bring? What are my choices?"

I pull out the pocket knives first and flick them open and closed, then slip them back into place.

"That's it?"

"No." I pull the gun from the front pocket of my sweatshirt and casually hold it at my side.

"That's better."

"I'm glad you approve. Now talk."

"Are you going to hurt me to get the information?" He looks way too happy about that.

"If I have to."

"You do," he affirms. "I know my fate, and what a beautiful fate that is." He grins. "But I don't have it in me to go down easy."

"I get that." Stepping inside the cell, I let the door close behind me and raise the gun. I take a breath, and on the exhale, I pull the trigger, shooting him in the calf.

Hovan lets out a mix of a grunt and laugh, keeping his jaw tight.

"You know," I start, "I never considered myself a violent person until recently. But I think it might just be because I was never given the chance. My father wanted to keep me a good little girl who minded herself and was chaste and pure for a husband. I was made to believe I couldn't go anywhere or do anything. But you know what?"

"What?" he says through a clenched jaw.

"All it took was being pushed too far for me to realize what I was willing to do to have control over my life."

"I've always preferred my women spicy, not sweet," he says in a taunting tone.

Blood soaks the mattress under his leg, and I point at it with my gun. "You better start talking."

"For every shot, you can have an answer. Leo took my

phone, but it won't have The Ghost's number on it. I used a disposable phone for that."

I pull out my phone and open my notes app. "What is it?" I ask, then type in the number he prattles off. "How do you know the hit came from inside my family and not the Cicariellos?"

"Ah, ah, ah, you have to shoot me again to get another answer."

"You're deranged," I sneer. "Why do you want this to be the way you die?"

"Throwing compliments at me will get you far, honey. So, I'll answer that question without a bullet. And the answer is because it turns me on. My dick got hard just seeing you holding that gun. But having you shoot me..." he trails off, humming. "I like the pain, and I can imagine you fucking me as you killed me. I have a vivid imagination."

My nose scrunches up in disgust. He's absolutely foul.

"Not the answer you were expecting, was it?"

"No."

"Good. I like to surprise my women."

I shoot him in the same leg again, right below my last shot. "I'm not even remotely close to being one of your women." I hate to even think about what that would be like.

Choking out a laugh, he seems completely unbothered by being shot twice. "I know it came from within the family because Joey Cicariello told me a while ago in passing during a deal we were making. He said he received an anonymous note telling him when and where he'd find Michael Carfano to take him out. Michael was notorious for his secrecy and safety precautions when it came to his whereabouts. So if

Joey received advanced notice where he'd be, then it had to have come from someone who knew his schedule."

He's not wrong. My father was a very cautious man when it came to traveling anywhere and being out in the open.

"I see that you know I'm right."

"Did he know who it was?"

His smile comes slow. "Who are you hoping it wasn't?"

"I'm hoping it wasn't anyone," I tell him, not willing to share my thoughts with him.

"You're a good liar, Katarina."

"Who was it? If it was sent anonymously, then how do you know?"

Studying him, I can see it written right there.

He doesn't know who it was.

"You don't know, do you? You just thought you could get me to kill you as some kinky fantasy."

He holds his arms out like he just won. "She gets it."

"You're fucking disgusting," I say in a rush, hating that I even came down here. He played me.

I would shoot him and kill him out of spite, but I don't know if the number he gave me is legitimate, and I sure as hell am not letting him take pleasure in his death.

He laughs like I'm the funniest person in the world, and even after I leave the cell and lock it, I still hear his manic laughter in my head as I put everything back that I took.

SHIT!

Now I have to find a way to tell Leo that I came down here *and* shot him twice…

CHAPTER 27

Katarina

Should I call the doctor for him?

I don't want Hovan to bleed out if Leo needs him alive.

There's no cell service down in the basement, but on the ride back up to Dante, I decide that it's not my call to make.

I see Dante sitting up in bed with the TV on, and I take a deep breath so I'm ready for whatever he has to say.

His head whips to me when he hears the door open, and his eyes roam over me to make sure I'm okay. "I woke up and you were gone."

"How long have you been up?"

"An hour maybe."

"Oh, I went to shower and change and..." I pause,

229

looking everywhere but at him.

"What happened?" His voice changes, dropping to a dangerous octave. "Katarina, look at me."

"I did something I probably shouldn't have and now I don't know what to do."

"Katarina, look at me," he repeats, and I finally meet his hard gaze. "Tell me what happened."

"I went down to see Hovan to ask him questions about what he said to me earlier, and I...well I..." He's looking at me expectantly, and I sigh. "I shot him twice in the leg. The opposite leg of the one I already stabbed him twice in last night."

Dante's eyes widen. "What the fuck, Katarina?"

"I needed to know! He's the one who wanted to play some sick game where I had to shoot him in order for him to answer a question. So I did." I shrug.

"What did he tell you?" he demands, and the harsh bite of his tone has me flinching.

"He gave me the phone number he used to get in touch with The Ghost. He said it wasn't on the phone Leo took from him since he used a disposal."

"What else?"

I cross my arms over my chest. "He told me the hit had to have come from inside the family because my father was so careful with his security, and he's right, Dante. He said Joey Cicariello let it slip one time when they were doing business that he received an anonymous tip on where to be and when in order to kill them. The only way someone could have known that is if they're in the family and knew his schedule ahead of time."

I walk the length of the room and then turn abruptly. "Dante, I think Leo had our father and uncle killed so he could take over. So that all of them could take over. I know our father was an asshole, but I didn't think Leo would do that. How can I face him now? The Cicariellos may have pulled the trigger, but Leo might as well have done it himself. It would've been more of a power move if he just took him out himself."

Dante looks like he's in pain, so I rush to his side. His eyes are pinched closed and his lips are pressed into a thin line. "What's wrong? Do you need more pain medication? Just press the button."

"No, it's not that," he rasps.

"Then what is it? Because if it wasn't Leo, then someone else in the family is vying to be boss and Leo might be next."

"STOP!" Dante yells, making me stumble backwards. "Just stop."

I'm completely stunned where I am. I've never heard him raise his voice before, and I have to hide my shaking hands by crossing my arms and balling my hands into fists at my ribs.

Dante peels his eyes open to first look at the ceiling and then at me. They're dark and unreadable as they swirl with too many things for me to catch even just one to hold onto and decipher, and I get a flashback of fear, like how I felt when he'd look at me when I was younger.

"It was me."

CHAPTER 28

Dante

Those three condemning words leave my lips and there's no going back.

I couldn't take hearing her go on and on about thinking it was her brothers, but now she's looking at me like she doesn't know me. Like she's afraid of me.

"Don't look at me like that, babygirl."

She still doesn't say anything. She just stares at me, wide-eyed.

Fuck this.

I rip the IV from my arm and pull the gel stickers from me that are monitoring my vitals, and sit up, dropping my legs over the side of the bed to face her. Her eyes widen even more and she takes a step back.

Pain laces through me, and it's not because I just tweaked my side and pulled at my stitches. I can take anything in this fucking world, but not her afraid of me. Not anymore.

"Don't do that, Katarina."

The floor is cold under my feet when I stand, and because I haven't used my legs in over 24 hours, they're stiff, but they could be broken and I'd still just crawl to her.

"Don't back away from me like you're afraid." I match each of her backwards steps with ones of my own until she hits the wall.

I stop a few feet from her.

"I had your father killed, Katarina. It was me. Not your brothers or anyone else in your family. Me."

Her throat works around a swallow. "Why?" she whispers.

"Because he was going to have you marry someone else. He never would have let me have you." I can still hear his condescending voice in my head. "He did a sweep of the security cameras and saw I was logging in remotely, and he connected the dots. He knew I was watching you even after he already warned me."

I take a small step towards her.

"He needed my skillset too much to actually kill me, but he needed to make his threat stick this time, so he left me with this as another warning." I point to the puckered gunshot scar on my left shoulder. "He said it was my last warning, though, and the next time he was going to kill me. And I knew there would be a next time."

Her hand raises like she wants to touch the scar, but then lets it fall back to her side. "He shot you?"

"Yeah, babygirl, he shot me. Point-blank. But I was already too far gone with you to give a shit." I take another small step forward. "There was no way I was going to give you up and let him hand you over to someone that wasn't going to love you like I could. To someone who was going to touch you and only give you a fraction of the pleasure I knew I could give you. And there was no way I was going to stay with your family and work for Michael if that happened. It was either kill him or be killed by him."

"What about uncle Sal?"

"He wasn't a part of the deal. The Cicariellos got greedy." I take another step closer. We're only six inches apart now. "Are you afraid of me, Katarina? You already know that I'm a killer. You already know that I've done things that would keep most people awake at night. You already know that I'm not going to stop doing those things."

"I know," she whispers.

"So, are you afraid of me, Katarina? Or are you afraid that despite what I just told you, you don't want to run from me?"

"No."

"To which question?"

"I'm not afraid of you." Reaching out, I brush the tips of my fingers across her jaw and she sighs, proving that fact. "But the way I feel about you has always scared me. It's always felt too intense and too big." She reaches out to touch the scar her father left me with. "I'm sorry he did this to you." Her beautiful honey-brown eyes dart between mine.

"I'm sorry he made you feel like you weren't good enough. Like you weren't worthy. He was wrong," she says fiercely.

"He wasn't wrong."

"You saved me from a life I never wanted, Dante. You're the only one who's ever truly cared about what happens to me. You're the only one who's ever *seen me*. You see past the mask I wear for everyone, and you actually find her…" she trails off, looking away.

"Beautiful? Smart? Capable? Powerful?"

"No, I was going to say that you actually find her desirable and worthy."

"Worthy of what?" I demand, not understanding what she thinks she could possibly not be worthy of.

She swallows hard. "Love."

I press myself fully against her, needing her to feel me as much as I need to feel her. "I fucking love you, Katarina," I tell her harshly, "and I've been a very selfish man about it. I've chosen you over everything. Even your father, who I owed my life to."

Katarina traces the scar on my cheek. I love it when she does that. "Then I'm selfish, too. Because if I was the one who had to choose between your life and my father's, I'd choose you. I wouldn't even have to pause to think about it, Dante."

My hips press into her and she groans, feeling my dick growing hard against her stomach.

She's perfect.

She was made to look and act like an angel, but think and react like a ruthless little fiend.

I fucking love her.

I slam my mouth down on hers, and the both of us groan on impact.

"You were made for me," I rasp, my control slipping.

"I know," she sighs against my lips, pulling me back down to kiss me with everything she has.

I feel it.

I can feel her obsession mixing with my own, until we're woven, tangled, and knotted together in a web we'll never escape. A web that will catch us and bring us right back together if one of us ever has a doubt. But as long as I'm alive, there won't ever be a doubt.

"We have to stop before I fuck you to show you how much you were made for me."

"Why?"

"Because I have to go down and make sure Hovan doesn't die before he tells me what I need to know."

"Oh, right," she sobers, realizing why she came into my room in a panic to begin with. She scratches her nails back and forth on my scalp and gives me one last kiss before patting my cheek. "I guess that asshole is more important than my need for you," she teases, and I groan, pressing myself flush against her — ignoring the dull pain radiating across my torso.

"No one's more important. You come first." I lean in and lick the shell of her ear. "In every sense of the term."

Katarina moans, and all thoughts of making sure Hovan doesn't die get pushed to the back of my mind. "Take your clothes off and bend over the bed," I order, and step back to watch her do as I say.

I lock the door and put the partition back in front of the

window and stand behind her. I run a finger down the line of her spine and she moves with me, arching and dipping under my touch like a cat.

Palming her ass, I rub her smooth skin until she's moving her hips with me and I stop, which has her whining in protest.

"You get what I give you. Understand?" She nods into the bed, and I squeeze her ass. "Use your words."

"Yes!" she says urgently, and I reward her with a hard slap of my hand to her perfectly round ass. She cries out again, then moans, pushing her hips back into me.

"I'm going to fuck you here first," I tell her, plunging two fingers into her already soaked pussy. "Then here." I drag my wet fingers up to rim her tight puckered hole. "Are you ready for that? For me to have all of you?" I press my middle finger to her small hole and push past her clenched resistance. I groan, her tight ring of muscles about to fucking snap my finger off. She nods her head into the bed again and I push my finger into her a little more, garnering a strangled gasp and moan. "Use your words."

"Yes!"

"Good girl." Pulling my finger out, I slap her ass again.

Pushing my boxers down so they fall to my ankles, I spread her ass apart and thrust into her pussy with enough force to push her up the bed.

"Grab the edge," I tell her in a rush, and she does so just in time for me to pull out and slam back inside. This heaven I thought for a split-second last night I would never get to experience again, calls to me now to be thoroughly fucked and used.

I pound into her, her pussy sopping wet and taking me like the good little cunt it is. Made just for me.

Gripping her ass harder, I lift her hips up and she cries out, her sounds muffled by the bed. With this new angle, I fuck her hard and fast until she's screaming, and my chest swells with pride that I'm the one making her pussy gush around me like a fucking dam just broke.

I pull out and swipe my fingers through her come, spreading it around her tight little hole. I continue to play with her pussy and rub her clit with one hand to keep her relaxed and distracted while I push my finger back inside her ass with my other.

"Dante!" she cries out, her hands white knuckle gripping the thin blanket on the bed.

I pump my finger inside her ass, moving it around to make room for a second finger, then spreading them apart to ready her to take me.

Fuck, she's going to strangle my cock.

Katarina shudders and shakes and then explodes a second time. Taking my fingers out of her, I slide my cock through her wet folds and position myself at her back entrance, pausing for only a second to savor the moment before pushing forward.

My cock is far bigger than my fingers, but she's going to take me.

With her come as my lube, I spread her ass cheeks and surge forward, my tip making it inside before she squeezes me and I can't go any further.

Fuck.

"Dante, I—" she says in a panic, and I reach around to

rub her clit so she relaxes again, and I'm able to push in another inch. She gasps, then moans, rocking back into me.

My baby wants more.

I push into her slowly as she continues to rock back into me until my entire cock is swallowed by her perfect ass. I pause to let her adjust to the intrusion, sweat beading on my forehead from the intensity of my need to pound into her and fill her last hole with my come.

I continue to rub her clit, her pussy dripping like a fucking faucet. "Dante," she moans, shifting her hips. "Please. More."

Her plea sends a bolt of lightning down my spine and I slowly drag my cock almost all the way out, pausing until Katarina's mewls and pleas for me to give her more are too much for me and I thrust into her.

She squeezes me and I lose my fucking mind.

I have no control left.

I take her ass like I own it, because I fucking do.

I want to tell her she's such a good girl for taking my cock the way she is, but I can't. The words don't come because I can barely think them, let alone speak them.

It's heaven and hell again, and with the way she's strangling me, I can't last much longer.

"Come for me, babygirl," I manage to grunt out between thrusts.

Pressing down on her clit, she turns her head to the side so I can hear her raw scream as she comes. She has a vice-like grip on me as I thrust into her one last time, stilling with her ass smashed to my thighs as I fill her with my come.

The deep and guttural groan that leaves me is that of a

fucking caged animal being set free.

She's mine.

All of her is mine.

Finally.

CHAPTER 29

Dante

"Stay right there," I tell Katarina, and she gives me a short grunt as a response, having been too thoroughly fucked to manage words.

I clean myself up in the attached bathroom and dampen a small washcloth for Katarina. I love that I make her so fucking messy with come that she needs me to take care of her after.

Flipping her onto her back, I take her hands and bring her to a sitting position. She groans, her eyelids heavy as she tries to keep them open. Lifting her chin, I kiss her swollen lips. "I love you."

"I love you, too," she says softly, and those words give

me fucking life.

I help her to her feet. "Hearing you say those words makes me want to fuck you all over again, but we have some business to take care of."

"You made me forget."

"I know."

"What if he's dead?" she asks, worried. "If he's dead and that number is fake, then Leo is going to be so mad at me and we'll all be sitting ducks until he strikes again."

"Take a breath, babygirl. Give me the number and I'll have Stefano run it." She grabs her phone from her discarded sweatshirt and hands it to me, just a single phone number typed out on her notes app. I take mine from the table beside the bed and call Stef. "I need you to run a number and tell me if you can get a trace on it. Fast."

"It's the middle of the night," he protests.

"It's supposed to be The Ghost's number and I need to know if it's legitimate."

He clears his throat. "Fine. But how did you get the number? I dumped Hovan's phone and found nothing. Did you go down there?"

"Just fucking do it and call me when you know."

Hanging up, I place my hand on Katarina's lower back. "Let's go. I need to get some clothes."

The pain meds are wearing off and I'm starting to think the slashes on my chest and abdomen are deeper than I thought because putting clothes on is a strained effort. I take a couple pills I still have in my bathroom from the last time I was injured and my phone vibrates on the counter.

"What did you find?" I ask right away.

"I traced the number to a room-by-the-hour, no questions asked kind of motel just outside of the city in Jersey."

"Do you know if it's him?"

"The place doesn't have an online system to hack since they cater to the hooker, trucker, and on-the-run crowd."

"We'll have to see for ourselves, then. Send out a mass message and tell everyone to get to the conference room."

"What's going on?" Katarina asks when I hang up, her eyebrows drawn together. "Is it his number?"

"It's a legitimate number, but we have to go and see for ourselves if it's The Ghost's," I tell her, pulling her in for a hard kiss.

"Should you be going?"

"I'll be fine," I assure her. "There's no way I'm not going. I need to be the one to kill him."

"You told me you'd be fine last night and you almost died."

"I told you I'd come home to you, and I did. Just like I'll come home to you when this is all over."

* * * *

"What the fuck is going on?" Leo barks when he walks through the glass doors. "You better have a damned good reason for waking me up like this, Stef."

"We do," I tell him, and he looks at me.

"Why are you here?"

"I found The Ghost," Stef says, typing away on his laptop.

"I thought you said there was nothing on his phone."

"There wasn't. Dante gave me a number to run. I found its current location at some cheap motel in New Jersey where there aren't any security cameras or a booking system to hack. But then I dug deeper and looked up what was around the motel and hacked the security systems of the surrounding businesses that show a partial view of the motel. It's him."

"How do you know?"

"There's a rental car out front that's registered under Hovan's name, and there's only one guy that's been coming and going on a regular basis for the past two weeks and has an Armenian cross tattoo. Which is ironic if you ask me for his line of work."

"How did you get the number?" Leo asks me, leaning back in his chair.

"He set me up last night, so I paid him a visit earlier," I cover for Katarina. "It took a little convincing, and a couple bullets, but he gave it up."

"What the fuck, Dante?"

"He's fine." I shrug. "For now. He memorized the number and used a burner."

He stares at me for half a minute, trying to gauge if I'm telling him everything. He has that way about him. Leo can read people better than anyone I know, but I'm also the master at hiding everything from everyone, so he has nothing to read.

"Coordinate a team to go and grab him. Or should I send Luca instead?"

"No. His death is mine."

Leo looks at me for another long moment and then

nods, standing. "Call me when it's done."

He leaves, and I start barking out orders to Stef to get his team together. As a captain, he has his own group of soldiers he's in charge of, as well as aspects of the business he handles. Gabriel and Marco have their own soldiers too, but I only need one team for this mission.

"They'll load up and be ready to go in forty-five minutes," he tells me, closing his laptop.

I want him captured before sunrise. I want to make sure we still have surprise on our side.

∗ ∗ ∗ ∗

I'm riding in one SUV with Stefano, and his team is in another as we chase the sunrise on the drive out to Jersey. The entire time, I have the image of Katarina being shot and falling to her knees at the forefront of my mind. That moment before I covered her with my body to shield her and I didn't think I'd get to her in time.

She looked at *me*.

It was *me* who she looked to in that moment, needing me to save her. She knew it was *me* who could protect her.

Before we left, I went over everyone's jobs, so when we arrive, we put our intercoms in our ears and I reiterate, "We go in quiet. Only use a weapon if needed. We don't need to have a cleanup crew called in if it's not necessary. You know your jobs. Let's go."

Flooding from the cars, two men go around to the rear of the motel to cover the window of The Ghost's room, with the other three on the team, along with Stef and I, taking the door.

He made the mistake of not realizing that he was seen coming and going from his room on the very edge of the convenience store's camera scope next door.

The pre-dawn sky gives us just enough light to operate as the lock is picked and we storm inside.

What the fuck?

It's empty.

The bed hasn't been touched and it looks like no one has ever stayed in here when I know for a fact he's been here. He was on camera last night returning to this room and hasn't left.

I look around and see a spy camera in the corner of the room, and nod to the door that leads to an adjoining room.

"Next door," I speak softly into the coms, signaling everyone to retreat back outside.

The lock on the door of the next room over is picked, and while the others draw their guns, I pull out my knife. The one coated in Katarina's come. She's here with me, and she's going to be with me when I slit this guy's fucking throat.

"Go," I order, but when the door is opened, I hear the click of a pin being pulled and pull Stef back just as a blast shoots off.

"Fuck!" he shouts, a hole the size of dinner plate now blown through the door and one of his guys bleeding out on the cement, having taken the brunt of the shot.

"Go!" I yell, and the other two men flood the room. Our presence is no longer a secret, so we only have a short window to grab him and get out of here. "Four and five, come around and grab three and put him in the trunk," I direct. It's easier to distribute numbers when out on a job. It keeps things short and simple.

Moving into the room with Stef, we find one and two fighting with The Ghost. With the way the sheets are messed up, I can tell we woke him, so we definitely had the element of surprise still. Two punches him in the jaw and one tackles him down to the floor while he's off-balance.

Flipping him over, one and two hold him down and zip-tie his hands behind his back.

"Get him up and in our trunk, and zip-tie his ankles too. I don't want that fucker trying anything."

Stef and I round up the bags of weapons and cash he has in the room, and start to hear room doors opening and closing and sirens in the distance.

I grunt when I lift two heavy bags onto my shoulders. "You good?" he asks.

"Just go," I grit through my teeth.

Tossing the bags in the back seat, Stef hops in behind the wheel and we take off just as police lights flash in our rearview mirrors.

I feel my shirt getting wet on the side and I press against it, my hand coming away with blood. Shit.

"Go to the vet," I tell Stef, and he looks at me sideways. "I told Leo he's mine. Go to the vet."

Stefano goes a half hour north instead of back into the city, bringing us to a small town that has a veterinarian's office we own. And not because we're such animal lovers. Their incinerator proves to be useful to us in situations like this when we need a body or evidence to disappear.

We turn off onto the uneven gravel drive and wind our

way around to the back of the property. The office is hidden from the road to ensure our privacy, and the incinerator is even farther back behind the tree line so it's not visible to the public when they park.

The Ghost has been pretty quiet in the back, which has me wondering what his plan is and what he thinks he can do to get out of this. Because there's nothing. Abso-fucking-lutely nothing.

We park and gather at the trunk. "Open it," I order, and three of our guys raise their guns while the other opens the trunk door.

The Ghost kicks his way out. He goes after our man with a knife, but Stef shoots him in each thigh, making him go down to his knees.

"You didn't check him for a weapon before you dumped him back there?" I growl at the team. *Fucking idiots.*

Kicking the knife out of his hand, I grab him by the throat and squeeze. "You shot my girl. You tried to kill her and her entire family, and you killed one of our men tonight." His face is turning red from lack of oxygen. "You made a mistake coming here. This is my territory. This is my city. This is my family."

I release him and he gasps for air, but I don't give him time to. I take my knife out and hold it to his throat. "No one fucks with what's mine." In one quick swipe, I slice his neck open, arterial spray coating my arms and shirt. He grips the front of his neck, blood spurting out from between his fingers, all the while keeping his dead eyes on mine. A battle of wills that I've already won.

I watch the life leave his eyes, and when he collapses to

the gravel, I bark out, "Burn him until there's nothing left, then bring Joe back home."

Joe was dead about ten seconds after he hit the walkway back at the motel. He was a good soldier who knew his job and his place in the hierarchy, so he'll get a full funeral service, not the incinerator.

CHAPTER 30
Katarina

Where is he?

Dante's been gone for three hours and I haven't heard anything.

What if he's dead?

Panic sets in and I pour myself a glass of whiskey, gulping down a third of it in a single swig. I cough at the burn, but take deep breaths through it as it spreads warmly through me.

Sitting in front of the windows, I look out at the city, hoping Dante is out there and on his way home to me.

I can't call his phone again. I've already tried twice and I don't want to compromise whatever he might be doing, so all

I can do is sit and wait.

At the bottom of my glass is when I hear the door open, and I rush to it, my head spinning from the whiskey.

"Dante!" I call out, throwing myself against him. His guttural groan of pain has me gasping and letting him go. "What's wrong? What happened?"

Looking down, I see my arm covered in blood and look at him wide-eyed. "What happened?" I panic.

"It's not all mine."

"Take your shirt off. Let me see." He's wearing black, so I can't discern what might be his or not.

"I'm fine," he says, but when he unbuttons his shirt and pushes it apart, I see he's anything but.

"You tore your stitches open and you're bleeding. A lot. I need to call the doctor." Running to my phone on the counter, I call him quickly and tell him to come here instead of the medical suite. "Sit," I order, and he leans on one of his kitchen stools. "I'll be right back."

Running to the bathroom, I grab his first aid supplies and hurry back to the kitchen. "You called the doctor already."

"I know, but I can't do nothing. You're hurt."

"Babygirl," he rumbles, and I pause, looking up at him. "I'm fine."

"Stop saying that. You're not. And besides, how would I know? You didn't call me to say everything went okay. You just let me sit here and worry while you went after some famed Albanian assassin."

I'm rambling, and Dante quiets me by pinching my chin. "Next time I'll call you. I didn't think about you worrying.

Come here," he demands softly, and I lean in, kissing him like it's our last one, holding his face in my hands. He slides his tongue across the seam of my lips and I open for him, his tongue sliding against mine in a fevered dance that only gets hotter and hotter.

"Did you get into my whiskey, babygirl?"

"Mm-hmm," I hum, licking my lips and diving back in for more.

We're broken apart by a quick knock at the door and I run to answer it in a daze. "Hi, doctor. Thank you for coming so quickly. Dante opened his stitches and he's bleeding."

"Alright, Miss Katarina. Don't worry, I'll take care of it."

"Thank you," I say, relieved.

Turning one of the living room chairs to face the kitchen so I can watch without being in the way, the doctor cleans and disinfects the stab wound, stiches him back up, and puts a fresh gauze covering over it. "Try to take it easier this time," the doctor says to Dante, but he just glares back. He doesn't like being told what to do.

"Thank you," I say for Dante. "I hope we don't have to call you again," I add, and he leaves quietly.

I lean on the closed front door and look over at Dante, his dark eyes hooded and on me. "Come back here."

"Tell me what happened."

"He's not going to be a problem anymore, Katarina."

I breathe a sigh of relief. "Good. Is everyone okay?"

"No, we lost one."

I bob my head, my mind thinking only one thing. *I'm glad it wasn't him.*

"I told you I'd come home to you," he says. "And there

was no way I was coming home without making sure the man who hurt you was dead."

My heart twists in my chest, loving how overprotective, vicious, and vengeful he is when it comes to me.

Kissing the spot below my ear, he whispers, "You were with me. I used the knife."

I grip his hair tighter, my body lighting up knowing he used the knife that was inside of me to kill him. "You'll have to take me back down to the targets after you clean it."

Dante groans, his teeth scraping my ear. "I fucking love you."

"Prove it."

"You're not going to insist I take it easy like the doctor said?"

"Oh, the only part of you I need is your mouth and your hands. I think that counts as taking it easy, don't you?"

"Hop up on the counter, baby. I'm starving."

CHAPTER 31

Dante

"Hovan, you know your fate here, don't you?" Leo asks, walking around him.

"I do, but I was hoping that beautiful sister of yours would do the honors of finishing me off." He grins. "She has a way with weapons that I enjoy."

He looks like shit. He's lucky to have survived this long.

Leo's face thunders. "Shut the fuck up. You don't get to enjoy your death. In fact," Leo says, taking a step closer to him, "you should feel honored that I'm going to be the one to kill you myself."

"Oh, yes, my mistake," Hovan jokes, coughing. "I held on this long so that I could have you kill me without the fantasy your sister would give me."

Growling under my breath, I hold back from ending this myself, knowing that he's Leo's to kill just as The Ghost was mine.

"Your first mistake was hiring someone to do the job you were clearly too much of a coward to do yourself. Your second mistake was thinking we wouldn't survive. Your third mistake was sticking around afterward, not believing I would find out it was you behind it and then go after you."

He laughs. "Any more you want to add?"

"Yes," Leo hisses. "Your last mistake was trying to kill my brother in that fight. You're lucky Dante is a tough son-of-a-bitch to kill."

"It wasn't supposed to be him fighting," Hovan points out.

"Doesn't matter."

"I suppose not. I wanted someone from your family's organization to die. I didn't think you'd be there to see it. Just that you'd get the message that I was still here and still after you."

"It's over. We got The Ghost this morning, and now you. Your family is done, Hovan."

"There are more of us."

"Maybe. But our territory lines no longer exist. I've taken what's yours, and if one of the few that have survived up until now decides they want to step up and try to put the business back together, then I'll be right there to set them straight. The Aleksanyan family is done in my city." Raising his gun, Leo sends a bullet through the middle of his forehead.

Leo turns to me, and I can see the weight of one more soul on his shoulders. But that's the price he pays as the leader, and the cost of remaining at the top of the food chain when everyone wants to take what's yours.

"I'll make sure it's cleaned up," I tell him, and he nods, handing me the gun as he goes.

I call in the cleanup crew and tell them to make sure Hovan and all evidence of him ever being here is gone.

I have some calls to make now that this situation is taken care of.

CHAPTER 32
Katarina

"You want me to pack only *one* bag? If you want me to live with you, then I'm going to need more than just a single bag of my things," I tell Dante, my hand on my hip. He brought me back to my old room and told me to pack a bag "As someone who has supposedly noticed everything about me for most of my life, I'm surprised you think that would keep me satisfied."

Growling, Dante pulls me against him and spins me so he has me pinned against the entryway of my closet. "I know how to keep you satisfied, babygirl," he says low in my ear. "And I would never ask you to pack just one bag. Because trust me when I say by the time we get back from where we're going, everything you own will be in our apartment."

"Our apartment?"

"Yeah, babygirl. *Ours.* I'm going to have the walls knocked down between the apartment Leo put you up in and mine to make ours."

"What? Why?"

"Because I want you to have a whole room for your things. Fuck it, make it two rooms. I want you to have whatever you want, Katarina."

"What if I don't want more space? What if I just want to be close to you?"

He growls again, and his hand on my hip tightens while his other slides up my chest to circle my throat. "I'd say that's the best fucking thing you could ever say to me."

"What if I also said I wanted you to fuck me on the bed I've spent countless hours lying in, fantasizing about you and how you'd touch me, kiss me, and take my virginity?"

I can feel his cock hard between us, and I bite my lip, rolling my hips against his. He groans, his breathing getting heavier. Inhaling, he glides his nose across my cheek and presses his forehead to mine. "Tell me one of your fantasies."

"I wanted you to show up in the middle of the night, waking me with your hands or mouth. You'd tell me to be a good girl and be quiet so I didn't wake my parents. And when I couldn't be quiet, you'd shove my face in a pillow to muffle my screams. I had no idea what it would feel like, any of it, but I knew you'd make me feel so good. I knew the dark side of you would give me rough, but I also knew from the way you looked at me, you wouldn't actually hurt me."

Dante presses his entire body to mine, letting me feel all

of him. "Interesting," he rasps, his lips brushing mine, "I fantasized about the same thing, babygirl." Kissing me hard, Dante plunges his tongue into my mouth and I'm eager to meet his, needing to be as close as possible to him and tangling us in a hot dance that makes me forget everything but him.

He squeezes my throat and pulls me away from the doorframe, leading me to my bed by the neck and not breaking our kiss until he pushes me away and I land on the end of my bed. His eyes rake down my body and his teeth scrape over his bottom lip after his tongue. "I'm going to give you your fantasy, babygirl."

Tearing my clothes off, Dante stands above me. "Get under the covers," he instructs, and my heart flutters in my chest. I crawl backwards and slip under the sheets, his heated eyes following me, filled with lust and love.

It's my turn to watch him as he takes his clothes off, and my chest pangs when I see the red slashes across his chest and the big bandage still on his side.

He's such a strong and resilient man, and I know he wouldn't tell me if he was in pain.

"Hey, look at me," he says, and my eyes lift to his. "I see what you're thinking, so stop."

He can't know what I'm thinking. "Stop what?"

"I see it written all over your face. I'm not hurting, and even if I was, I wouldn't go easy on you right now, babygirl. Got it?"

"Yes," I sigh, gripping the edge of the comforter.

Dante pulls the top sheet and comforter free from between the mattress and box spring, and I rub my legs together, my core throbbing. Right before he disappears under them, he gives me a look that holds a thousand secrets and a million promises, all of which I want to know and experience.

Crawling under the bedding, my heart skyrockets, practically beating out of my chest. He touches my ankle and I jump, my body wound-up in anticipation.

His hands glide up the sides of my legs as he plants open-mouthed kisses in a trail up the fronts of my shins and thighs, alternating between my legs. I can feel him but I can't see him, and I sigh with every kiss, not knowing where his lips will press to my skin next.

Reaching the tops of my thighs, he pauses, inhaling my sex with a groan and then surprising me with the slashing of his tongue across the top of my mound. Moaning, my legs part automatically, and Dante takes advantage by pressing my thighs to my sides and slashing his tongue through my pussy this time.

I cry out, my hips flying up to meet his mouth while my hand slides under the sheets to grip his hair. Dante grunts and goes in for a second swipe, swirling his tongue around my clit until I'm a sobbing mess and begging him for more. But just as I'm about to find bliss, he breaks the hold I have on his hair and continues to kiss his way up my stomach despite my protests.

"You're going to have to be quieter if you don't want your parents to wake up and find me in here. That's my death sentence."

I moan, squirming under him, loving that he's playing into my fantasy. I bite my lip and pinch my eyes closed, trying to be as quiet as I can as he traces the underside of my breasts with the tip of his tongue.

"Dante," I sigh, and he shushes me, blowing cool air over my nipples, making them painfully hard.

Tweaking one with his fingers, he captures the other in his hot mouth and my back bows off the bed. I slide my fingers through his hair again and hold his head against me.

He goes back and forth between my breasts, and I can only take so much before my eyes water from holding back and trying to be quiet.

"Please," I beg, my voice shaky. "Please, Dante."

"Shhh," he hushes, twisting both of my nipples and licking a path up the front of my throat. "I said don't make a sound, babygirl."

"It's hard. Please, Dante."

"You make it hard," he rasps against my lips, pressing his hard cock against my core. I can't hold back my moan when he rocks his hips, and he captures it for himself with his lips. "You make me hard, Katarina. Every time I see you and think of you, I'm hard. It was a very painful time when I couldn't have you."

"You can have me now," I whisper.

Growling low, Dante tilts his hips back and aligns himself at my entrance. "Nothing and no one will keep us apart anymore, Katarina. No one will make you do anything you don't want to do, and I'll always put you first. Understood?"

Tears fall from the corners of my eyes to the pillow under my head. "I know you love me," I manage to whisper through my tight throat. "I love you, too."

His eyes flare and he surges his hips forward, entering me in a single thrust, burying himself inside of me. We groan together, and I wrap my arms around his shoulders, clawing at his back to get him even closer.

Dante pulls out of me slowly, and then drives forward, my pussy clenching around him, loving the feeling of him filling me past the point of just fitting. He stretches me, letting me feel every inch of his width, and he hits a spot deep inside of me, letting me feel every inch of his length.

"You don't have to be quiet anymore, babygirl. I need to hear your sounds. I need the music of our love."

That was sweetest thing he could've said, and when he pulls out of me and surges forward again, I'm not quiet. My moan fills the room and he snaps, kissing me hard as he fucks me harder.

Each thrust of his hips has his tongue plunging into my mouth and I can only take so much before I tear my mouth away and bury my face in his neck, gasping for air.

Dante kisses my neck — sucking, licking, and biting his way up to swirl his tongue around the shell of my ear.

I claw at his back, the sounds leaving me making Dante fuck me that much harder.

"Come for me, Katarina. Let me hear you scream. Let this entire fucking house hear you scream so it knows who should've been fucking you all along."

My inner muscles flutter, and when Dante bites down and pulls on my earlobe, my body is engulfed in flames and I scream my release, raking my nails across the width of his shoulders and down his biceps.

Dante continues to pump into me through my release. "I

can't stop," he says. "I can't stop, babygirl. I don't want to stop."

"Please," I sob, feeling the pressure building within me again.

"You're going to come again," he demands roughly, his gravelly voice in my ear sending a shiver down my spine and making my pussy squeeze him in return.

He palms my breasts, pushing them up and together. "Now," he commands, twisting my nipples.

I scream, the sound echoing in my head as I explode again. But I still have too much I'm feeling inside of me that I need to get out, and I sink my teeth into the curve of Dante's neck to give him some of the crazy I'm feeling. I have nowhere else to put it but into the man causing it.

He groans, stilling inside of me and filling me with his hot come, coating my insides with his love.

My vision blurs and my eyes roll back into my head, my body not able to take anymore.

"I still need you to pack a bag," Dante mumbles into my neck when I come to. "But first we need to shower."

Lifting me from the bed, Dante carries me to my bathroom and walks me right into the shower where he takes his time washing me, and I him. We dry off and I rebandage his side with fresh gauze before getting dressed.

I'm in my closet pulling out a few things to put in a suitcase when Dante comes up behind me, looking at my rack of dresses. "I like this one," he says, pulling out a floor-length blush pink dress that has a corset bodice covered in pearls and crystals.

"Me too." I smile. "I tried it on for fun one time and didn't want to take it off. So, I bought it." I shrug.

"You should pack it."

"Seriously?" I say with a short laugh.

"Yes, seriously."

"Will I need it?"

"Does it matter?"

"I suppose not," I conclude, and place it in a garment bag with matching shoes before going back to packing more practical things, but making sure to include a few extra sexy things to surprise Dante.

When I'm all packed, he takes my suitcase and garment bag and brings them down to the car. "You're still not going to tell me where we're going?"

"No."

Sighing, I look back at the house I grew up in. It's by far not the last time I'll set foot in there, but now I have the best memory to dull some of the worst ones that reside inside those walls.

My mom is allowed to come back here now that the business with Hovan and The Ghost is taken care of, but when I called her yesterday and told her about Dante and me and how I was going to live with him, she said she was going to extend her stay in Miami and then go and spend some time at our villa in Italy.

She deserves to live her life and create beautiful memories for herself outside of this house.

I thought she was going to have a lot to say about me

and Dante, but instead, she told me she hoped I found the happiness she never had and that she was proud of me for standing my ground.

When we hung up, I broke down and cried while Dante held me. I didn't realize I wanted my mom to approve of my choice so badly. But I did.

I'm going to have the life she never got to have.

CHAPTER 33
Dante

Katarina has no idea what I have in store for her. I talked to Leo and Luca in person with Alec included on conference call the day after Leo took care of Hovan, and told them how I wanted to surprise Katarina. It took a few days, and the help of Abri, Angela, and Tessa, but it's come together.

"Are you almost ready?" I ask Katarina, adding cufflinks to my sleeves.

"You know, you should never rush a woman," she calls back to me from the bathroom. "But you're in luck, because I am ready." She steps into the bedroom and I swear to fucking God, my heart stops.

She's stunning.

Absolutely stunning.

She takes slow, deliberate steps towards me, the dress I told her to pack and then insisted she wear tonight is painted on her body. "That dress was made for you, babygirl."

"You like it?" she asks, the look in her eyes telling me she already knows the answer.

"I fucking love it."

She graces me with a smile that's so sweet, I know if I were to kiss her right now, she'd taste like candy. "You don't look so bad yourself, Mr. Salerno," she purrs, adjusting my tie. "So handsome," she says softly, her honey eyes telling no lies. "You must be surprising me with something special tonight if you got us both dressed to the nines like this."

"You'll see," is all I say, and she gives me a sexy little grin, pressing her lips to mine in a soft kiss.

"Oops." She wipes her thumb over my lips. "I got a little gloss on you."

I lick my lips and catch her thumb, biting down. Wrapping my arms around her, I pull her in for a real kiss, wanting her to know I plan on kissing her always, lip gloss or not. "Now we're ready," I tell her, licking away the gloss from my lips.

We're staying in a presidential suite at The Aces, the Carfano's casino in Atlantic City, and I place my hand on her lower back as we head down to the casino floor. All eyes are on Katarina as we walk, and for once, I don't mind. In fact, I would be mad if they *didn't* look. She's radiating light like the damn sun, and everyone is drawn to her, making it impossible to look away, and I don't blame them.

We walk the perimeter of the casino floor, around where the shops are for people to blow their winnings, and stop outside of Carfano's, the family's Italian restaurant.

"Before we go in there, I want you to know how much you wanting me, and choosing me means, and I'm going to spend my life trying to be worthy of you."

"You don't have to prove yourself, Dante. I already told you I just need you. You're enough."

Taking her hand, I bring it to my lips and kiss her knuckles. "I love you."

"And I love you," she says sweetly. "I'd love you even more, though, if you told me were going inside to eat. I'm starving."

"Not yet. We have to do something first." Taking her hand in mine, she looks up at me, slightly confused, and then stops short when she sees the restaurant doesn't look how it usually does.

The tables have been moved out and the chairs are arranged in rows with a wide aisle down the middle, leading to a massive arch made of white and light pink flowers in front of the stone fireplace.

Her entire family is already seated and waiting, including her mom in the front row. Abrianna, Angela, and Tessa made sure flowers are fucking everywhere, and from the look on Katarina's face, I can tell she likes it.

"Dante, what's going on?" she asks, her eyes wide.

"You told me you'd marry me, babygirl."

"I did," she agrees.

"So you're marrying me. Tonight. Right now. It may not be a big wedding, or a fancy one, but I'm not waiting another day to have my ring on your finger and yours on mine."

She looks up at me, her honey eyes melting for me. "It's perfect. I never wanted a big wedding. I always knew if I did have one, it was going to be planned by someone my father or Leo hired and would be some massive production to show everyone how well we're doing. This is me. This is beautiful. I love it, and I love you," she gushes. "But I don't have a ring for you."

"Already taken care of."

"How did you do this? When did you do this?"

"I had help," I tell her, and the three women responsible emerge from the back of the restaurant.

"Kat, you look amazing!" Abri squeals when she sees her, and Tessa and Angela give their own praises. "And Dante," she says, looking me over. "You look like a scary James Bond."

"Abri!" Katarina laughs, and the corner of my mouth lifts in a smirk.

"Thank you." The three of them stare at me as if I have two heads, but I know it's only because I haven't said more than ten words to each of them since I first met them. "And thank you for helping me with this."

"Of course," Tessa says, smiling wide. "We were excited to. Anything for Kat."

"It's beautiful, thank you so much. I had no idea," she says.

"We know." Angela smiles, and Leo, Alec, and Luca come out from the back next.

"You look beautiful, Kat," Alec tells her, and she hugs all three of them.

"Thank you for being here for this. For us," she says, coming back to my side and sliding her hand into mine.

"Kat," Leo starts, clearing his throat. "I know we've had some difficulties over the years, and especially recently, but I was wondering if you would let me walk you down the aisle?"

Abri smiles at Leo and Katarina dabs at the corners of her eyes. "Yes, I'd like that."

Abrianna hands Katarina a bouquet of flowers and Leo leads her to the restaurant's entrance where we have a few men posted to make sure no one interrupts our private event. Alec, Luca, and I take our places on the right side of the arch, while Abri, Tessa, and Angela stand on the other side, each with a small bouquet of flowers

I told the girls they could do whatever they thought Katarina would like, with only two requests of my own. A lot of flowers for Katarina, and I wanted a violinist playing "Nella Fantasia" while she walked down the aisle to me.

The violinist begins the song and everyone stands. Katarina's aunts, uncles, and cousins all turn to watch the most beautiful woman in the world walk down the aisle to me.

Me.

Dante Salerno.

The fucking Executioner who's killed too many to count and even had her father killed. And yet here she is, walking towards me and looking at me with love in her eyes that reflects mine.

When they reach me, Leo kisses his sister's cheek and gives me her hand. "Take care of her. Or you know what'll happen."

"I know."

Katarina smiles up at me and I feel it all in that smile. My entire world is standing in front of me and I take her hands in mine, the vibrations of her life flowing into me, giving me more notes for her song. She's all I'll ever need in this life.

The moment we both say 'I do' and we slip our rings onto each other's fingers, I bring her in for a back-bending kiss that lets everyone here see that The Executioner has one weakness.

Katarina Carfano.

ACKNOWLEDGMENTS

A massive thank you to everyone who has read and loved my Carfano men and the women who bring them to their knees. Now, you've gotten the Carfano woman who brings her man to his knees. Dante has been living rent free in my head for two years, and I couldn't wait to bring him to life and let you all know why he is the way he is.

Thank you to my family for always believing in me and being there to celebrate in both my small and large victories, as well as picking me up from the lows that are inevitable in this author life.

ABOUT THE AUTHOR

Rebecca is a dreamer through and through with permanent wanderlust. She has an endless list of places to go and see, hoping to one day experience the world and all it has to offer.

She's a Jersey girl who dreams of living in a place with freezing cold winters and lots of snow! When she's not writing, you can find her planning her next road trip and drinking copious amounts of coffee (preferably iced!).

newsletter, blog, shop, and links to all social media:
www.rebeccagannon.com

Follow me on Instagram to stay up-to-date on new releases, sales, teasers, giveaways, and so much more!
@rebeccagannon_author

Printed in Great Britain
by Amazon